"Twenty thousand dollars is a lot of money, Mr. Tremayne. You wouldn't mind telling me just what it is you want me to do, would you?" she asked.

His chuckle was low and sexy. His eyes when he turned to her were full of laughter. "Do you think I come to auctions to hire my mistresses, Ms O'Donald?"

She gave him a lazy smile of her own in return, though her palms were feeling damp. "Somehow I don't think you pay for mistresses at all, so you must want something else. A lot of something else."

"You're right, Ms O'Donald. I need someone to put in long hours in various capacities, working around the clock at times. So the job will entail accepting board and lodging at Tremayne Hall, but I can assure you that it's honest employment I'm offering."

His voice was low. For one heart-stopping moment when he looked d̶o̶w̶n̶ ̶a̶t̶ ̶h̶e̶r̶ ̶s̶h̶e̶ was going to k̶i̶s̶s̶

Myrna Mackenzie, winner of the Holt Medallion honouring outstanding literary talent, has always been fascinated by the belief that within every man is a hero, inside every woman lives a heroine. She loves to write about ordinary people making extraordinary dreams come true. A former teacher, Myrna lives in the suburbs of Chicago with her husband—who was her high school sweetheart—and her two sons. She believes in love, laughter, music, vacations to the mountains, watching the stars, anything unattached to the words *physical fitness* and letting dust-balls gather where they may. Readers can write to Myrna at PO Box 225, LaGrange, IL 60525-0225, USA.

Recent titles by the same author:

PRINCE CHARMING'S RETURN
BABIES AND A BLUE-EYED MAN

AT THE
BILLIONAIRE'S BIDDING

BY
MYRNA MACKENZIE

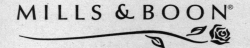

To my niece, Christy Henley,
and my nephew, Marcus Mackey—
We all have stars, big and small, that we reach for in life.
Best wishes on catching a few stars to hold in your hands.

*First published in Great Britain 2001
Harlequin Mills & Boon Limited,
Eton House, 18-24 Paradise Road, Richmond, Surrey TW9 1SR*

© Myrna Topol 2000

ISBN 0 263 82520 5

*Set in Times Roman 10½ on 12¼ pt.
01-0701-48787*

*Printed and bound in Spain
by Litografía Rosés, S.A., Barcelona*

Chapter One

"That's him. The new owner of Tremayne Hall. Look. No, don't look *now*. He'll see you."

Gideon Tremayne smiled at the whispers buzzing around the crowd on the grassy area of the Eldora town square.

The whispers continued. "He's rich." "The descendant of a knight—or something." "With lots of women all over the world." "More women than any one man could possibly need."

Gideon raised one brow at that mild exaggeration as he took a seat in the back row of folding chairs that had been set up on the lawn.

"You're wrong, love," he said beneath his breath, noting the elderly woman who had made the comment and who was staring at him from behind her raised program. A man couldn't have *too* many women—not when they were such fascinating and lovely creatures.

In fact, it was his need for a woman that had brought

him to the Third Annual Summerstaff Labor Auction for Charity. He'd just this morning gotten an e-mail from his sister Erin with some unsettling news, and now, unexpectedly, he was going to need some assistance. He hoped he could find it here.

But he could see from the program that the one lady with all the qualifications he wanted wasn't due to make an appearance until farther along in the auction.

Gideon stretched his long legs out in front of him and prepared to wait. He smiled and nodded at the elderly woman and her friends, who were still trying to peer at him while appearing not to be looking at anything. They smiled back, fanning themselves furiously with their programs. Finally they turned their attention to the temporary stage in front of city hall.

Gideon looked down at his own program. He wondered which one of the ladies milling about on the lawn was Caroline O'Donald. He tried to match a face and body to the somewhat fuzzy picture in the brochure.

No luck. For a few seconds, he wondered if she wasn't even there, if she'd withdrawn for some reason—or perhaps changed her place in the order and he'd somehow missed her.

His hand tightened on the brochure slightly. Erin was so wounded since her fiancé had left her, and now she'd lit on this misguided idea of helping him that was doomed to failure. It was clear the thought of scheming to save him from himself was making her happy, which was what Gideon wanted.

He definitely didn't want Erin to feel she was failing again, but he didn't plan to change his life-style for anyone, even an ''anyone'' he adored. He needed to somehow reassure her that he was satisfied with his life. Unfortunately, words just wouldn't be enough. He'd been giving her words for some time now. She needed proof. He needed a plan—and a woman to help him demonstrate his contentment. He hoped the person in this brochure was as good as she sounded, because it was already the second week in June. With only two weeks left to prepare before his sister's visit, time was too valuable to waste.

What's more his presence here was proving too much of a distraction for the audience. The noise and head turning was increasing.

"Wouldn't be polite to disrupt the auction, Tremayne," he whispered to himself, slipping from his seat and wandering farther afield to a tree-lined area still within view of the stage. He probably could watch from here without attracting too much attention, he thought, crossing his arms and leaning back against a tree.

Then he finally saw the female he'd been seeking. She was less than ten feet away, standing in the middle of a group of women, a dreamy smile on her lips.

Gideon studied the lady closely. Her picture, he saw now, was a damned unsatisfactory substitute for the real thing. She was taller in person, almost regally so. Her auburn hair was longer than he had imagined, her mouth more generous, her blue eyes more striking. She was wearing a short, straight, white silk dress, and his gaze automatically dropped to her legs. Long. Lush. An unexpected streak of heat slithered through him.

An inappropriate streak, he reminded himself. Her legs were none of his business. He never chose his women from his employees, and he never chose them for the long-term. That wouldn't be fair when he was incapable of giving what every woman had a right to expect. As for this woman, she had a right to certain expectations, too.

"The right to know that she's wanted for your business, not your pleasure, Tremayne," he told himself, trying to ignore the unexpected ache that Caroline O'Donald had already called forth in his body. A woman should never have to worry about an employer's unwanted advances.

Gideon struggled to put his thoughts in the right place. Then the lady looked at him. Her already wide blue eyes looked startled. He could almost see her taking a deep breath. Gideon wondered if she was a mind reader, or if she could see the heat literally rolling off him in waves. He had an awful urge to yank his tie off and pop open the top buttons on his shirt. And he had an even greater urge to pull her close and cool his skin with her own. Judging from the way her chin rose high at that moment, he had the feeling that he was doing a damned poor job of hiding his reaction to her. It was not like him to be so transparent, and he fought his all-too-male response to her. He tucked his alarming thoughts away where they belonged.

But by then, the moment was over and she was turning away, slowly and with great dignity. As if she had dismissed him completely. As if she were a queen.

"Perfect, Ms. O'Donald," he whispered, relaxing, letting the tree support him as he stretched his legs out farther in front of him. The decision had been made. Caroline O'Donald was the ideal woman for this job, and he meant to have her.

* * *

"Almost time to join the party," Caroline whispered to herself, as she stood at the base of the stairs awaiting her turn on the stage.

"You're not even nervous, Ms. O'Donald?"

The young usher's voice broke into Caroline's thoughts and she turned to the girl with a reassuring smile.

"Oh, this is the third summer I've done this, and most of the time I just go out there and pretend I'm Miss America," Caroline said with a grin. "Without the crown and roses, of course. Or the tears. But to me, this is fun. I'm what's known as a hands-on teacher over at Alliota Junior High. I love putting on a show. We check the references of every employer to ensure the workers' safety, so that's not a worry. Besides, my friends, Rebecca and Emily and I organized this auction. It's for a good cause."

And it was. The auction had been born when one of their students had needed medical attention that the child's parents couldn't afford. Helping out had just been natural, especially since working at a school meant their summers were free. They'd recruited other teachers easily, since all the wages went to needy kids. And in a good-size town like Eldora, there were plenty of employers to go around. She loved doing this.

And, ordinarily, she would have been rushing onto that stage. Just a few minutes earlier she would have. When Emily, one of her two best friends in the world, had gone to the town's Romeo, Caroline had been impressed. Now, after finding herself the object of that disconcerting, gorgeous, gray-eyed man's attention, she felt off balance. It was an unfamiliar response, this urge to hang back and let the others go ahead of her.

Not that she would. She'd never be that cowardly.

"Hey, don't worry about me. I'm fine, angel," she said, sending the girl off for a much-needed break. And she *was* fine. This would be a good summer. She'd always been the kind to make lemonade out of the lemons life had given her, and although she'd made oceans of the stuff in her thirty-one years, things had been looking brighter lately. Ever since last winter when her latest love, Donald, had skipped out forever, and she'd finally decided to drop out of the love and dating scene, life had taken a turn for the better. She intended to keep it that way. No temptation or involvement. Just safe, dull work this summer, nothing to threaten the fragile peace she'd found for herself.

"Hey, Caroline, you're on," Rebecca, her other best friend, said, stepping to the edge of the stage and smiling at her. "You okay? You're looking a bit pale."

Caroline wrinkled her nose and smiled back. "I'm always okay, Becky. You know that."

Her friend looked even more worried. "I know you're a treasure. The crowds love you. Remember that, okay?"

"I'll remember," Caroline assured her friend, who was last on the list of those to be auctioned off. "But I'm really perfectly fine. You know I love being on a stage, and knowing I'm helping kids really fires me up, so don't worry, hon. See you on the other side."

Of course, she *did* love this event, Caroline reminded herself as her friend melted into the background. Just because that sinfully handsome man had momentarily made her remember her idiotic and annoying tendency to jump in feet first and let her emotions run down the road didn't mean she was going to do that this time. Oh no, because if anyone had learned that romance was seriously dangerous to a woman's happiness, she had. From now on, she planned to aim for something more comforting and attainable. She wanted a man to give her children, not heart palpitations. And hey, she thought with a smile, she'd done just fine. She'd seen the man, she'd admired. Nothing wrong with that. She'd have to be a block of limestone not to notice the guy was ten kinds of temptation in a suit. But she hadn't done anything stupid. And now she was ready to go out there, enjoy herself, and earn some money for the cause she loved.

Caroline stepped out on the stage. ''Good morning, Eldora,'' she called.

The crowd called back.

She noticed the man leaning against the tree hadn't spoken. She also noticed he had the kind of dark, longish hair most women would love to feel brushing against their bare skin, that his shoulders were broad beneath his white shirt and dark suit, and that he was studying her from beneath half-lowered lids.

But what did that matter to her? She was here to find a job and earn some money for kids who needed it. And he was probably just a spectator. He didn't look like the type who'd be cruising around for a baby-sitter or typist. And he wasn't really even sitting in the audience.

She smiled on. She waved to the crowd. She held out her hands to them.

''Thank you so much for coming,'' she called. ''I just want to say that we've all pledged to work our hearts out no matter how big or small the job may be, so…let's keep going.''

The crowd cheered.

In the background, Caroline could hear the auctioneer reading off her qualifications.

The man with the compelling eyes continued to study her with that lazy, assessing look. Her skin suddenly felt hot and tight. She was more aware than she'd ever been of the fullness of her lips, her breasts, the way her hips curved away from her waist beneath the clinging silk of her dress.

Oh, he was very good. She had to give him credit. The man knew how to use those eyes and that body language. Too bad for him that she was beyond temptation. She was one safe puppy. So Caroline decided to enjoy the moment. She raised the wattage of her smile. She thought of all the children this auction would help. Then she turned to the side slightly, staring right back at the dark-haired man wearing that lazy, come-to-bed-sweetheart look. He was, after all, just a man.

And then, unable to resist, she gave him a wink.

The crowd noticed, and roared.

The man's lips turned up at the corners and he saluted her with a slight bow of his head. He winked back and the gesture made him look deliciously wicked. Sexy. A man who, no doubt, knew many things about the ways to please a woman.

For one ridiculous second, Caroline felt dizzy. Crazy. As if she, who never blushed, might be blushing.

And then, as the auctioneer started the bidding, Caroline lost herself in the show. Someone offered two thousand dollars for a stint helping at the local teen center. Another person topped that by two hundred fifty dollars to win her as a private tutor. Some good-natured ribbing ensued.

Caroline relaxed, happy to let her remaining tension go and pleased that her summer would be spent on something worthwhile.

Then she sensed movement to her left. The dark-haired man had raised one long finger. He nodded to the auctioneer before looking her straight in the eye.

"Twenty thousand dollars," he said, his voice low and hushed in the sudden stillness as he held her gaze. He didn't bother stating his purpose.

Caroline knew she looked startled, because the man's lips lifted ever so slightly. As if she amused him.

But she was no longer amused. The man had just bid an obscene amount of money for her, even more than Emily's Romeo had bid, and with absolutely no provocation to go so high. What on earth did that mean? She hoped it didn't mean she'd given him the wrong impression. She'd certainly traveled that road before—and traveled it badly.

A stunned silence hung over the crowd. Four seconds, five. And then as if everyone had finally found their voices, a chorus of startled murmurs filled the air with noise.

The auctioneer looked askance at the audience.

The audience looked over at the man who shrugged and smiled engagingly.

"The timing isn't the best, but allow me to introduce myself," the man said, in a deep, quiet voice. "I'm Gideon Tremayne, and I've only been in Eldora less than two weeks. Most of that time has been spent setting up my new offices, but I'm certainly looking forward to living here and meeting as many of you as I can. For now though, sir..." he said, turning to the auctioneer "...shall we continue?"

The auctioneer grinned and looked out over the audience. "Anyone want to raise the bid...? No? That's it then. It appears she's all yours, Mr. Tremayne."

"All mine? Then I'll be sure to take very good care of her," Gideon said, pushing off the tree in a fluid, graceful move and walking toward the stage where Caroline still stood.

She stared straight into the eyes of the man who had bought her, and swallowed hard. She knew that name. In a midsize town like Eldora, it was impossible to know half the people, but this man was a bit different. He was wealthy. His grandfather's business ventures for England had inspired the queen to confer knighthood on him. His father had bought the house everyone called "the palace," a few years ago. And Gideon himself was the reason Paula Masters had left her position as his maid when she'd fallen in love with him after only five days on the job. The woman had cried loudly and publicly before she'd left town—just two days ago.

But that was none of her business, Caroline reminded herself as the crowd grew louder. However, why a man would bid twenty thousand dollars for her *was* her business.

She looked around at the smiles and winks. She listened to the roar his announcement had made.

"Well, you certainly know how to liven up an auction, Mr. Tremayne," she said, forcing a lazy smile of her own.

He tilted his head in acquiescence. "I'll take that as a compliment, Ms. O'Donald. Shall we go?"

He held up his hand to help her from the stage.

She looked at the long, strong fingers, followed the line of his arm up to his shoulder and stared straight into those amused, gray eyes. Eyes that made a woman want to do wild, wanton things she'd never done with a stranger before. Pleasurable things. In the dark. With a bed beneath her back.

Caroline swallowed and closed her eyes for a second, trying to beat back her thoughts. She would be in some kind of trouble here if she didn't really watch her step.

But she would. She had to. She'd sold her time to a man with blue blood, a man who probably made women beg with desire, and one who had already broken one local woman's heart.

"Is there a problem, Ms. O'Donald?" he asked, his deep voice vibrating through her body.

She stared him straight in the eye.

"I've never held hands with the grandson of a knight before," she said, masking her nervousness with humor.

He smiled. "Neither have I, Ms. O'Donald, but I can assure you that my hand is no different from any other man's."

She could have argued that point, but to what purpose, Caroline thought, looking down to where he still waited, hand extended, knowing her hesitation was beginning to draw attention.

So she plunged in. She placed her hand in his and felt his warm fingers close over her own. She did her best to ignore the intensely erotic feel of his skin against her own. She had, after all, been many things, but never a coward, and she wouldn't be one now. That didn't mean she wasn't relieved when she reached ground level and he released her. Still…

"Twenty thousand dollars is a lot of money, Mr. Tremayne. You wouldn't mind telling me just what it is you want me to do, would you?'' she asked, as they walked away from the crowd.

His chuckle was low and very sexy. His eyes when he turned to her were full of laughter. ''Do you think I come to auctions to hire my mistresses, Ms. O'Donald?''

She gave him a lazy smile of her own in return, though her palms were feeling damp and her breathing slightly labored.

''Somehow I don't think you pay for mistresses at all, and I'm clearly not mistress material, so...'' she held out her hands, ''...you must want something else. A lot of something else.''

''You're right, Ms. O'Donald. I want a lot of something. I need someone to put in long hours in various capacities, working round the clock at times. So the job *will* entail accepting room and board at Tremayne Hall, but I can assure you that it's honest employment I'm offering.''

''Room and board? You don't mean that I'll be staying at the palace, do you?''

Gideon raised both brows. ''The palace?''

Caroline smiled sheepishly. ''That's what we called it when we were kids and the Evershams still lived there. You have to admit that it looks like one. Even if it doesn't have a moat.''

He lifted one corner of his lips. ''How remiss of the original owners not to have installed one. And yes, I do want you to stay there for the next three or four weeks.''

''Alone?''

His eyes seemed to darken slightly. ''I'm sure we'll be hiring other people.''

She nodded slowly. She gave in to her urge to grin. "Fine then. I've always wanted to see the inside of—"

"The palace," he supplied with a grin of his own.

"Yes. I must have wished on a star for that very thing at least a thousand times."

"You're a very romantic woman, then?" His words were accompanied by a frown. She couldn't blame him. She didn't at all like the thought herself.

"Oh no, Mr. Tremayne. I hope this job doesn't require anything too fanciful, because you won't find any woman less romantic than I am." It felt good to say the words.

It must have felt good to hear them, too, because an intense look of satisfaction crossed his face. Almost the way a man looked after a passionate night with a woman.

Stop it, she told herself. *Just stop it right now.* Just because she hadn't been involved with anyone for months and had deprived herself of physical contact, didn't mean she could indulge herself now. She couldn't allow it.

But then he took her hand in his own again. "You'll want some time to pack?" he asked.

She managed to nod.

"Then I'll expect you in two hours, and we'll begin." His voice was low. For one heart-stopping moment when he looked down, she thought he was going to kiss her hand.

But then he stared at her fingers lying against his own, and he released her.

She cupped her fingers, still warm from his touch, against her side as he turned and waved.

Thank goodness she was no longer that romantic, impetuous woman she'd once been. It was so good to know she'd left all that nonsense behind. Because if she hadn't, she might be in for some very rough waters. Gideon Tremayne was very definitely a man who could be dangerous to a woman's good intentions.

Chapter Two

"So this is what grandsons of knights drive," Caroline said as Gideon handed her out of her car. His silver Porsche sat in the drive next to her obviously old subcompact.

He shrugged and smiled. "I haven't checked with the other grandsons of knights, so I'm not sure what their transportation requirements are."

"How about their employee requirements?" She raised one delicate brow. Gideon had to give her credit. The woman didn't beat about the bush.

"You want to know exactly why I hired you. Well, the situation is a bit more complicated than I'd like," Gideon said as he led her to the stone steps outside Tremayne Hall.

"I can deal with complicated. Most of the time."

Her voice was soft and Gideon looked down at the woman standing by his side.

Wide, blue eyes stared back at him. Beautiful eyes. Make-love-to-me-this-very-minute-and-never-stop eyes.

He covered his own eyes with one hand, wiping away the fantasy image. Where had that thought come from?

"I guess I should probably tell you something about myself right now, Mr. Tremayne," Caroline said, as she stopped at the top of the wide stone landing. "The thing is, that, well I'm trying to behave and not look like I'm dying to bombard you with a billion questions, but I'm just not known for being a real patient woman. Maybe it would be best if you just hit me with this twenty thousand dollar mission right between the eyes."

The slight laughter in her voice made him smile. She *had* been patient, and she was being a good sport. He wondered if that would change once she knew all he wanted from her.

"All right, I'll be blunt, Ms. O'Donald. I need a miracle worker here." He smiled down at her.

She raised her brows. "Any particular type of miracle?"

His smile turned to a grin. "Well, for starters, my house is a complete mess. I've been traveling for months, I still have rooms of boxes to be unpacked, and now I need to have the place in perfect order in less than two weeks."

"You want *me* to set up *your* house?" She moved with him as he opened the door and gestured her inside. Stepping over the threshold, her eyes lit up like a thousand glowing candles.

"Oh, it's magnificent," she said, spreading her arms out from her sides and turning as she craned her neck to look up at the high ceilings and the stained-glass skylight overhead. "I've seen the outside many times, but I always knew it would be even more beautiful inside. Everything's so…big, with all this gleaming wood and marble. And that sweeping, curving staircase is like something out of a child's storybook. Mr. Tremayne,'' she said, beaming up at him, ''do you have any idea just how lucky you are?''

At the moment, gazing at Caroline's face, aglow with what looked like ecstasy, Gideon did know. He wondered how many men had earned the privilege of seeing her this way.

But that was irrelevant, none of his affair now or ever. He forced himself back to the topic at hand.

''I—thank you, Caroline. I rather like this place myself.'' And he did. It was the only one of his father's properties where the man hadn't housed a mistress. Edwin Tremayne had died only weeks after buying it. He'd been convinced that Eldora, an easy drive to both Chicago and the rolling hills of the Galena Territory, Ulysses S. Grant's Illinois home and a haven for tourists, would be a prime investment for a real estate baron.

And now Caroline O'Donald was in love with his home, Gideon thought. Maybe she was even more right for this task than he'd realized at first.

''So you really want me to help with your house?'' she repeated, as if she'd won a prize and needed to be pinched.

''As much as possible in just over two weeks. I hear you know something of old houses and how they work.''

She laughed. ''You could say that. I come from a big family. Five kids and almost no money. We all learned how to repair almost everything, simply because we had to.''

He nodded his approval. ''Even so, this is a big task, I'm afraid. Loads of unpacking, sorting, decorating, and almost no time to do it in. You may be working night and day at times.''

''What happens in two weeks? Does your long-awaited bride appear to inspect the premises?''

''My bride?'' Gideon almost choked, but he held his smile, for her sake.

She looked suddenly embarrassed, and shook her head. ''I'm sorry. When we were kids we used to make up stories about this place. Forget what I said. You're fixing it up so you can stay here, of course.''

Gideon took a deep breath. He looked directly into her eyes. ''I'm planning to stay,'' he agreed, ''but that's not the reason for the rush. I'm expecting guests.''

''*Is* there a bride?'' she asked, wide-eyed.

He couldn't help chuckling then. ''No brides, Caroline. I'm just not—that is, I'm sorry to spoil a good childhood story, but I'm afraid that in spite of my ancestor's title, I'm not the stuff stories are based on. And I'm definitely not husband material. Some people just aren't meant for marriage. No, it's my sister who's coming, and she's bringing friends. Women. Two of them.''

''Ah,'' she said softly, and he suddenly felt like a little boy caught doing something he shouldn't.

''Ah?'' He widened his eyes, crossed his arms and stared down at her, rocking back on his heels. ''What does that mean?''

''It means it's clear your sister doesn't realize you're not going to marry. She's bringing the women for you, isn't she?''

He shrugged. ''She might be. Oh, hell, Ms. O'Donald, of course she is. Erin is a worrier. She's two years older than me, and even though I'm thirty-three, to her I'm still her baby brother. When our mother died last year,

I sold the family home, since Erin and I disliked it, and I began to visit my other properties. I've been on the move a lot, selling off some houses, commissioning others to be refurbished. She thinks I'm neglecting myself, that I need a woman's touch. And since her engagement ended, she's been at loose ends. Her fiancé hurt her. I don't want to hurt her, too, but—there are limits.''

''You can't just tell her you don't want to get married?''

''She knows that, but she thinks I'll change my mind if she introduces me to the right woman. And frankly, even if I convince her I don't want to marry, which I will, I suspect Erin will insist on staying here to take care of me. This is, after all, her home too, as far as I'm concerned, but I think that would be a tremendous mistake. I'm far less worried about the other women than I am about Erin. She needs something new to hold onto, and I don't intend to let her give up her life for me. I'm not going to let her hide here because she's afraid.''

''So how do you intend to stop her?''

Gideon opened his mouth to speak, then closed it again. He stared down at the beauty standing before him.

''I want her to realize I don't need anyone to help me manage my life. I saw in the Summerstaff brochure that you've headed up more social events than anyone else listed. You've been involved in college and community theatre. You've mentored the drama club for the last five years at the junior high.''

''Somehow I doubt you're asking me to stage amateur theatricals in your home. So...'' She looked up at him. Waiting.

He blew out a long breath. ''Okay, the complete twenty thousand dollar mission. Besides organizing the house, I want you to be my hostess, Caroline. I want you, in fact, to become completely at home in this house, to be the lady of my life for a few weeks. In a very formal, nonphysical, friendly sort of way, of course. We don't need to pretend it's permanent or even real. If she knows where I found you and that this is just a job, that's fine. I just want her to realize I can fill the role of lady of-the-moment whenever I need to. My world can run smoothly, my home can be comfortable, and my social life can be full without benefit of a wife or a full-time caretaker.''

Caroline's eyes were growing wider by the second. She held out her hands, which trembled ever so slightly.

''You want me to be your hostess. And these friends—are they—are they wealthy like you? The social cream?''

He tilted his head. ''I suppose so. Yes.''

''Of course,'' she said, as if she were talking to herself. ''They've been raised in luxury.''

Ah, he could see where this was going now. She was struggling to hide her distress. One lock of her hair had caught on her lips when she'd shook her head and the temptation to gently push it back in place was great. Itchingly so, but he stopped himself from touching her. It wouldn't do for him to initiate anything close to personal. He'd already somehow hurt one woman in his employ. He wasn't sure how. He hadn't even been attracted to Paula Masters, but somehow she'd thought he wanted her and had cried when he'd found her work elsewhere. He certainly wasn't going to risk taking advantage of a woman working for him the way his father would have. He would watch his every move. So, slowly Gideon curled his fingers into a fist. He backed away from the thought of touching Caroline. He tried to remember what they'd been discussing. Oh yes, her concerns about becoming his hostess.

"Caroline, you've hosted larger functions." He pulled the Summerstaff brochure from his jacket. "Don't you read your own press releases?"

She stared at him as if he'd just lost every ounce of sense he'd ever possessed.

"Gideon, what were you thinking when you bid on me?" she asked, holding her hands out in supplication. "Of course I know what that brochure says. I wrote it myself, and it says that I've hosted PTA luncheons, awards nights, pep rallies, and church socials. None of those qualify me for what you're suggesting."

Her voice shook slightly. She was obviously fighting nervousness like mad, so he ignored his orders not to touch. He took her hand in his own, his thumb stroking slightly, stilling her movements. "You charmed the crowd today, lady. Completely."

"It's not the same," she insisted.

"You'll do fine," he said soothingly. "I'll help you."

Caroline felt Gideon's skin against her own, the repetitive motion of his thumb circling against her palm and for a moment all her thought processes gave way to pure sensation. But then reality returned with a jolt. She jerked her hand away. What did this man want from her? Did he have any idea what he was asking? She was Caroline O'Donald. She'd been alternately termed a tomboy, a wild child, and a woman far too impetuous for her own good. She had never, ever, been called a sophisticate.

"Gideon, I am not what you're looking for. You want someone who knows something about your world."

"I want someone who *looks* at ease in any situation."

She pulled back, grasped his arms and looked deep into his eyes. Big mistake. Their gray depths were a sensual trap.

"Gideon, do I look at ease right now?"

He grinned back at her.

"Actually, Caroline, you do. Almost. Another woman would be shrieking or fainting or walking out the door."

"I'm getting there."

"To the shrieking and fainting?"

She looked down her nose at him as best she could, given the fact that he was several inches taller than her.

"In just a few minutes I'll be walking out the door."

He slowly shook his head.

"How are you going to stop me?"

"I just paid twenty thousand dollars for your time. You owe me, Caroline."

"Maybe you just want to donate it?" she asked, her voice ending on a higher note than she'd meant it to. "You're a rich man. You must donate money to good causes all the time."

"See how well you're handling yourself? Who else would have the nerve to suggest such a thing? And yes, I'm rich, and I'd love to make a sizeable donation, but I'm not the problem, Caroline. I'm afraid you've given me the impression you're a woman of your word. I was sure I heard you say you'd work your heart out no matter what the job was."

"And I will. I would—but you can't want me for this. I know what I am, and I'm not what you think."

"Then we'll work with what you are. You're what I've got, Caroline. Erin's only thirty-five. I don't intend to see her bury herself here, and she'll try. So forgive me for playing dirty, Caroline, but do you want to just let a good woman attempt to throw her life away? Do you want that kind of thing on your conscience?''

Damn the man. She looked up into those compelling gray eyes and she was ready to give in to anything. All right, she would do it, and it would just be a part like many she'd played before. She'd clean his house, decorate it, and then she'd play the role of his chosen lady. It was for a good cause, after all. It was for a fellow female who'd gotten her life trampled by an unfeeling male just the way she herself had now and again.

She crossed her arms and looked Gideon directly in the eye.

''All right, you've got yourself a paint-by-numbers-hostess, Gideon. I'll do my best to work your miracle.''

His answering smile could have turned an ordinary woman's heart into a river of melted chocolate.

Good thing she wasn't an ordinary woman. From now on, she was Gideon's hired hostess. And no mere man, not even one with eyes of gray smoke and a voice that could charm most women out of their nightgowns in January was going to affect her at all.

So, she was going to be a trooper, Gideon thought. She was looking determinedly cheerful, and he wondered if that was Caroline's usual demeanor. Probably so. After all, she'd taken his twenty-thousand-dollar bid in stride when it had literally come out of the trees. And the way she'd winked at him when he'd been staring at her told him she knew how to make the best of a touchy situation. She'd made the crowd feel good that there was a human being on stage they were going to bid on. He'd just *bet* she was the kind of person who would comfort the police officer who'd just written her a ticket, or pat the hand of the doctor giving her a shot.

And now, here she was in his house, alone with him. Not a comfortable situation for her, he was sure. He wondered what rumors were flying about Paula Masters, or what she'd heard about his father's tendencies. The thought that any of this might be adding to her discomfort made him more determined than ever to help her feel at home here.

"All right, Caroline, why don't I show you your room so you can get settled in before dinner?" Gideon offered, picking up her bag and stepping forward to lead her toward the stairs.

But she tipped her head back and stared up at the massive double staircase. "I suppose I should, and I don't mean to sound dazed or naive, but I have to tell you—this is so…wild," she said, looking up to where the sunlight was streaming in the floor-to-ceiling windows at the upstairs landing. "Somehow I can't help thinking I'm going to wake up any minute and Bobby Cummings is going to be laughing at me, pulling my ponytail, and telling me that the day an O'Donald gets to stay in a place like this is the day Eldora sinks into the ground."

Gideon couldn't help chuckling at her slightly wounded expression.

"Sounds like he was a charmer. How old were you then?"

"I was twelve and Bobby Cummings was the first boy who ever kissed me. He did it pretty well, too, for a twelve-year-old."

Interesting.

"Was that before or after he pulled your ponytail and insulted you?" he asked, smiling.

She shrugged and looked up from beneath long, dark lashes. "He made that comment *after* I wiped off his kiss and kicked him in the shins, so maybe he had some justification. Wounded pride, I guess."

Gideon grinned. "I see you had your mind turned against romance at an early age."

"No, I just didn't want Bobby to know I had a tremendous crush on him. He was the boy every girl in sixth grade was drooling over, and I was probably the tenth girl he'd kissed that week. Just another conquest, so I couldn't let him know I'd been envious of the nine girls before me up until that minute." Her soft laughter was bright and lovely and sparkling.

But the woman was forbidden, he reminded himself. He should definitely take a lesson from Bobby Cummings and learn to keep his mind off her. Tremayne Hall and its master were about to effect a change. He wasn't going to repeat the mistakes of the past. No tangling in the sheets with an employee, no matter how enticing she sounded or how sweet she would probably taste.

"So what happened to your charming young man?" he asked, backing away from the thought of licking Caroline's lips.

She firmed out those pretty plump lips and shrugged. "Oh, he got Nancy Jessup pregnant and they married and had four kids. He manages the theatre in town now. Actually, I think he's pretty happy. But *I'm* here," she said with another laugh. "So lead the way, Gideon. I've braced myself. My dreams are about to come true. I'm standing at the bottom of the grand staircase of Tremayne Hall and finally ready for the tour. Just let me clear the stars out of my eyes so I can see better.''

She sounded as if this really was the dream of a lifetime, and for a moment, Gideon felt hesitant. Ridiculous, he knew, to care what she thought of his home. The lady was an employee, like any other. Except that wasn't quite true. She would be living here. In a few weeks, she would be standing by his side. His hostess and his ''lady'' for a week, even if he was paying for the privilege, and she was just an example to prove a point. Of course she would be *only* that. This was all a carefully arranged scenario. He intended for even Erin to know that much.

''So what if the reality doesn't live up to the dream, Caroline?'' he asked, motioning to their surroundings. ''This place has been uninhabited for a long time. A skeleton staff to clean and inspect it now and then, of course. I'm partial to my home, but it's been empty, it's old, and now it's filled with the trappings salvaged from a dozen other Tremayne houses. I wouldn't want to burst a childhood bubble.''

She shrugged. ''You won't. I'm not *really* expecting it to live up to my girlhood dreams. Most of my ideas back then were pretty impractical anyway. For awhile I wanted to be Tarzan's Jane. And then I thought it might be nice to be a trapeze artist and fly with some muscular guy who'd catch me every time. The palace was my greatest fantasy, but it *was* just a childhood dream. Anyway, this will still be a treat and an adventure.''

''In that case, I'll give you the full grand tour.''

''The whole thing?'' She was practically dancing from foot to foot.

''Dungeons and all,'' he promised.

She wrinkled her nose at him. "Don't think you're going to scare me off."

He shook his head. "I have the feeling you don't give in to fear easily, Caroline. Here goes."

She trailed him around the first floor, where only a few of the main rooms had been cleared. Her eyes widened at the massive dining room, the kitchen that could supply an entire platoon of guests with food, the roomful of computer equipment he called an office, and the gold parlor with the huge fireplace. They peeked in on the still-waiting-to-be-decorated library, the blue parlor, the morning room, the gallery, the conservatory and the ballroom. Then they went upstairs.

"Not much open up here, I'm afraid. Just the master bedroom suite—and one guest room."

He saw immediately that he'd made a mistake. He should have cleaned out another room this morning, something farther down the hall. Right now the only extra room available was the one right next to his.

"We'll get someone in here to help you tomorrow," he said, placing her bag in the room. "You can choose whatever room you like. There are plenty available."

Caroline took a deep breath and smiled. But he could see that she was working hard at putting on that shiny front she seemed to manage most of the time.

"No problem. I'm an adult, Gideon."

That, of course, was the problem. She was very much an adult, an enticing bundle of cheer, dark lashes, lustrous long hair—and a body that could make a man agree to fry in hell for eternity just for the chance to touch her for a single second.

And until Erin arrived, he and Caroline would be in the house alone at night.

He took a bracing breath, nodded toward the deepening darkness at the other end of the hall.

"The views from some of the other rooms are fairly impressive. You might like one of them." And he might like to spend the night downstairs in his office until they worked this situation out.

Caroline nodded, looking at the distance between his door and hers.

In spite of Eldora's size, she probably *had* heard something of Paula, but he didn't know what that was. What he *did* know was that he didn't want her to have a sleepless night.

"Tomorrow we'll open up more of the rooms. In the meantime, I've got lots of work to do tonight and I'll probably sleep in my office. If you need something, you'll have to come find me. Do you remember the way?"

She nodded. A slightly looser smile reached even her eyes this time, and he was glad he'd made that decision.

He wished he'd been this aware when he had hired Paula as a maid two weeks ago. If anyone should have been, it was him, given his past and his father's hunger for the women he employed. As it was, Gideon thought, he'd been so involved in setting up his office he didn't really remember much of what had gone on. He still didn't know what he'd done to lead Paula to believe he'd wanted something he hadn't, but she'd obviously expected him to respond when she'd come into his office that morning and offered herself to him.

A vision of his father with his hands up the housekeeper's dress rose up before him. He'd only been eleven years old at the time, and it had been a cruel awakening. Especially when Miss Devins, who had seemed more like a parent to him than his own, tearfully told him she needed the money his father gave her for her favors. He'd promised himself then that he'd never wield that kind of power over another human being. He chose his partners carefully, women who welcomed the limitations of his heart—and he hadn't repeated his father's sins.

But Caroline couldn't know that. This town wasn't so large that news didn't travel. It was obvious from the auction today that some news about him had traveled just fine. Maybe more had, too, and if he and Paula were being discussed, then the fact that he'd found the woman another job was probably being seen as a payoff for services rendered.

He opened his mouth to speak, and then closed it again. What, after all, was there to say?

"I'll leave you to your unpacking," he said gently. "And see you downstairs for dinner at seven?"

She nodded. "Do you mind if I wander?"

Her chin was raised high again. Good. She'd gotten past that nervous patch. "Wander away. This is your space for the next few weeks. And Caroline?"

She tilted her head and waited.

"I meant what I said. Choose any room you like."

She'd probably choose the one farthest down the hall. If she had any pity or sense, she'd do just that.

Chapter Three

Caroline sat at the long table, around the corner from Gideon and tried to calm herself. This house was entrancing, and yet she was clearly out of her league—with this man, with this place, with this position and certainly, when the time came, with his sister and her guests. What on earth had led the man to believe she was capable of pulling this off?

And how was she going to keep ignoring the fact that every smile Gideon gave her sent a shimmy of warmth up her spine. Every move he made—heavens, just watching the man breathe did awful things to her insides. And he was a master breather.

And so, okay, she was attracted. He was, after all, a treat to look at. And to listen to.

But that was just too bad. She wanted to be comfortable, to relax, to be herself. She did not want to let some misplaced attraction spoil this opportunity. So she *would* be herself. She'd do her best to enjoy this unique situation. Could be fun. After all, when on earth would she ever again get the chance to work for a millionaire and live in a mansion like this?

And so Caroline gathered her courage. She hazarded a look at Gideon who was looking very striking in black and white.

He must have felt her gaze on him, because he turned and smiled at her as an elderly servant entered the room. The woman stood for a second, gazing at Gideon, a maternal smile transforming her face as she presented him with his meal.

Caroline beamed at the lady.

The tall, pear-shaped woman looked from Gideon to Caroline and shook her head. She placed the other plate in front of Caroline, then left the room, jostling the door on her way out.

''So I see you're not completely without help,'' Caroline said, looking down at her plate which held something slightly resembling food.

''Not completely,'' Gideon answered, picking up his fork. He didn't seem to notice that the vegetables looked like they'd been cooking for the last decade and a half, or that the fish was singed on one side. ''Most of my time since I've been in town has been spent establishing an office for my business. Eventually, I would have straightened out the house, too. But Mrs. Williams does come in to cook and do laundry. The basics.''

Caroline hazarded a bite. The food was edible. Not appetizing, but apparently not deadly, either. Gideon studied her, smiling as she stared at her food.

''I needed a cook,'' he explained. ''The agency told me Mrs. Williams needed a job. I confess that my business has been my top priority most of the last few years.

And choosing menus has never been high on my list of things to do. Until my mother's death last year, she handled those details.''

Caroline had a slight premonition that Gideon's sister knew about Mrs. Williams and the gooey vegetables, and that was why she was so worried about him, but then, that really *was* between him and his sister. He'd hired his cook just as he'd hired her this afternoon. Not exactly a flattering thought.

''Your business—you said you've been selling off and fixing up your properties. Does that mean you're in real estate?''

He tilted his head. ''That's what the Tremaynes are known for, but that was really my father's contribution to the family funds. I custom design and troubleshoot computer systems. Tremayne Tech has offices in Chicago and Urbana. I'm just setting one up here. And I assure you, Caroline, that I spend more effort on my computer systems than I do on my meals.''

She couldn't help smiling. ''I'm sure Mrs. Williams is a sweetheart and she's grateful for the work.''

He chuckled and toasted her with his wineglass. ''I'm sure she thinks she's doing *me* a great favor by feeding me, and in fact, she's probably right. I needed a cook. Now I have one.''

''Lucky man,'' she agreed. ''A cook, a sister you adore and who obviously adores you, wealth, a thriving business, and a house right out of a picture book. What more could a man want—except maybe something to fill up all the space you've got in this house? Do you realize how many children you could have if you ever decided you were a marrying man? You could raise your own symphony orchestra, or your own baseball team.''

If the man could have sat up straighter or looked any more startled at that moment, Caroline would have liked to have seen it. His gaze locked on hers. A genuine look of shock passed over his handsome, even features.

''I'm afraid I'll have to leave those endeavors to someone else. Reproduction and child rearing just aren't a part of my plans.'' His voice was low, slightly strained.

''You don't like children?'' She couldn't help it. She leaned forward, studying him to see what she'd missed. She could believe he'd broken a local lady's heart. He was, after all, a man who could make a woman melt just by looking at her. But how could a man who grinned so easily not like children?

Gideon swiped one hand across his jaw. She sounded so wounded, as if he'd told her he tossed a baby out the window every morning just for fun. It wasn't like that. It wasn't really even her concern, but he had to work with her, and—hell, he just didn't like how easily he'd killed the laughter in her eyes. So he'd try to explain, and then maybe she'd see he wasn't a monster. He'd just chosen the best and only way.

''I wouldn't exactly say that I don't like children,'' he began. ''I don't have much experience with them, actually. What little contact I've had has shown me that the health and welfare of those who are young and impressionable shouldn't be left to people like me. Parenthood isn't something I'd be good at.''

''How can you know without trying?'' she asked.

But he knew. There were his own parents, after all. He was, he knew, in many ways very much like them—lacking the crucial "love and affection" gene. His father had been devoted to his business prospects, his mother to the business of maintaining the family name. Neither of them had any talent for, or interest in, raising children. And neither did he. The few experiences he'd had with kids, with his cousins and with the son of a woman he'd dated for a while, had been disasters. Children needed what he was incapable of. Love. Commitment.

He cleared his throat and looked directly at the woman waiting for an answer.

"I know enough," he said. Enough to know he wasn't willing to try and risk harming the heart of an innocent child in some sort of grand, self-serving experiment.

"But you, Caroline, you're a teacher. I'm assuming that, unlike me, you'd like to have a child or two."

"Oh yes," she said, brightening up, her eyes turning to pure glow. "And I'm going to have them, too. As soon as I can. More like four or five, though. I like big, noisy families."

He picked up his water glass and studied her. "But you say you're not romantic. Wouldn't that be a bit of an obstacle?"

At his question, she looked slightly flustered, but she shook her head.

"No, I don't think so. A woman doesn't need romance to marry and have children. And a good man doesn't have to be romantic. He just has to be kind, obviously willing to start a family. And he has to be somewhat...I don't know...reasonably virile? Capable of impregnating a woman?"

Capable of impregnating...her. The words rushed through Gideon's mind like a powerful waterfall, strong and unstoppable, slamming into him. The sudden vision of himself laying her down, peeling back her clothes, twining her legs about him as he slid deep inside her to seek his pleasure had him fighting to hold himself still, to try to find words. Any words. A voice that was close to calm.

He planted his palms on the table, drank in a slow breath of air, and risked a glance at her. She was looking a bit flushed herself, as though she realized just how foolish it was to say those words to a man like him. A man who'd never made any secret of the fact that he wouldn't marry, and that his times spent in bed would, therefore, be just for pleasure. From what he'd heard at the auction today, he suspected that the world knew that he liked pleasure. No doubt Caroline knew it, too, and was finally remembering that very thing.

"It's late," he said, rising to his feet. "You'll want to have some time alone, and I, as I said earlier, will be working." There, he hoped he'd set her mind at ease. No matter how frantic his need for a woman, he could be trusted to behave himself with her. When this was all over, he'd definitely have to end this too-long bout of abstinence. But for now, he'd fight the urge to feel the silk of Caroline O'Donald's skin beneath his fingertips. Taking a breath, he waited for her to join him.

She pushed back her chair. She dared to offer him her hand as if she didn't even see the danger in touching him.

He took it—and schooled his mind to focus on other things. Business. The Harmon account. How to get the man to see the sense in upgrading his system. There, almost there. He was barely feeling the softness of her skin beneath his at all.

"Thank you for dinner," she said. "And for giving me this job. This is going to help a great many... people."

Gideon tensed. She'd meant to say children and had stopped herself. She was going to be cautious around him now, when she'd been so open all day. The thought sent a spike of disappointment through his body. He shoved it away. She was right. She was one smart lady. He could take a lesson here.

"Would you like me to escort you to your room? The house is big. It can be dark if you forget where all the light switches are." He had to offer. Even if the thought of walking up the stairs with her toward the only two open bedrooms created an aching need in him that he refused to examine any further.

She slid her hand from his quickly.

"Oh, no, that's all right," she said, shaking her head and causing the lovely reddish strands of silken hair to tremble with her movement. "I'm not afraid of the dark, even if I can't locate the lights. I'll be perfectly fine on my own."

And he would be perfectly fine once he channeled his thoughts away from this woman.

Still he stayed to watch her walk away from him. He noted the way her hair swished against her hips and clung to her midnight blue skirt as she moved.

He wondered if he hadn't made a mistake in getting Paula another job.

Paula had wanted him, but at least the feeling hadn't

been mutual. She'd been good at her job, and even better, he hadn't felt any attraction. With her, he wouldn't have had to spend his time untangling his thoughts from visions of the woman in his arms, the way he was going to have to with Caroline. It was going to be a long few weeks. He only hoped that when those weeks were over, he would have what he wanted. Erin would be happy and back on track with her life, and he would be free to return to his own life; working, living alone, and sharing his bed with a willing woman when he chose to do so.

It was a good life, the kind that suited a man with emotional limits. He suddenly couldn't wait to reclaim that life-style. Until then, he would be celibate—and frustrated.

"Okay, Caroline, spill the beans. What is Gideon Tremayne really like and what does he want from you?" Emily asked her friend later that evening. The three of them were talking via a conference call that Rebecca had arranged. They'd already discussed Emily's new employer, Simon Cantrell, a member of the elite of Eldora, and they would undoubtedly soon bring up the subject of Logan Brewster, the hotel tycoon Rebecca had been auctioned to. So it was strange, Caroline thought, that she felt so fidgety and reluctant to discuss Gideon. The fact was that she didn't even want to think about him.

"Caroline?" Emily prompted again.

Caroline sat on the high bed and tried to forget that there was a big, beautiful man prowling around downstairs. She smiled at her friend's protective attitude. "Calm down, Em. He seems very…nice." What else could she say, after all? That he had a way of looking at a woman that made her want to shimmy out of her clothes to feel his naked skin against hers? Heavens no, she couldn't even think that.

"He's kind to his cook…and to me," she managed to add.

"Hmm…that certainly says a lot of nothing, Caroline," Rebecca mused. "And what does he want?"

"Well, he doesn't want to have his wicked way with me as you two seem to think. Right now he's sleeping downstairs so I won't feel uncomfortable being alone with him in the house."

"Okay, okay, I'm impressed," Emily acknowledged. "But what does he want you to do to earn all that money?"

"He wants me to transform his house into a showplace and hostess a house party."

"Sounds a little cozy," Rebecca said.

"I'll be fine, Becky love," Caroline assured her. "You know me. I always roll with the boat."

"But you've gotten involved with a lot of bad captains over the years," Emily reminded her.

It was true. Donald had wanted her for fun—for a while. And before him, she'd made Robert laugh, until he'd wanted someone less overwhelming. But those days were over. Those bee stings had healed and taught her valuable lessons.

"We just don't want you to get hurt, Sunshine," Rebecca said gently.

"I won't. I promise." And it was a promise she would keep. As the middle child in a big family, she'd made her way by learning how to attract attention to herself.

Now she'd simply have to tone that tendency down. Should be simple. And besides, she didn't want Gideon's attention. He wasn't a worry.

"The man's just too good looking for comfort, Caroline."

"He is that," Caroline agreed. "Makes your heart just start pumping something awful, doesn't he? But don't worry, I'll still be fine. And I'll tell you why."

"Well, it can't be that he doesn't like women."

"No, I'd say he likes women a great deal."

"You want to clarify that, hon?"

"Just a feeling," Caroline assured her. "Nothing he's suggested."

"Good. I'd hate to have to make mashed potatoes out of such a beautiful face."

Caroline smiled. "Thanks for worrying, Em. I'm really going to miss you two for the next few weeks." They'd gone through a lot together. A lot of pain, broken hearts, and fun. They all worried about each other, but she didn't want them to worry about her now. Not when they both had their own problems and somewhat sticky situations to deal with.

"Listen, you two, I want to tell you something. There really is nothing for you to worry about. I know that for sure because today Gideon mentioned that he doesn't want to get married."

"Not unusual in a good-looking male."

"And he doesn't want to have kids. Not ever," she added.

A second of silence made Caroline aware she was holding her breath while she waited for her friends' reactions. If she could take a load off their minds, she would feel so much better. Why have three people worrying when one person could easily handle that little trick all alone?

"Well then, he doesn't want kids. That *is* good news," Rebecca said, her voice already cheerier. "We know you too well, Caroline."

"And now we can sleep easy," Emily agreed. "Because if there's one thing Rebecca and I know, other than the fact that you are the most romantic, impractical, wonderful, giving person, it's that you would never fall for a man who wouldn't agree to give you a big family. Yessir, Gideon Tremayne can quirk his little finger all he wants, he can give you smoldering looks or take his shirt off right in front of you ten times a day, but he'll just be wasting his time."

Caroline swallowed hard at the image Emily had just projected.

"You're absolutely right, Emily." There was never going to be anything between her and Gideon Tremayne, Caroline agreed, as she hung up the phone a few minutes later. There couldn't be, not when neither of them wanted anything to happen.

But that didn't mean she didn't know just how tough these next weeks were going to be, Caroline thought, listening to the dark silence filling her room and wondering again what Gideon was doing downstairs. She was alone in this big, beautiful house with a man who had the annoying tendency to make her mouth go dry and her knees go weak just by entering a room. Or maybe just by being in the same building, she amended, realizing she was getting that weak-kneed feeling right now.

But if her knees were weak, at least her resolution was strong. She and Gideon were just going to work together. She could handle that. She was tough. Impervious to deep gray eyes and her own weak knees. And to make her point, she punched her pillow into a ball as she lay down and waited for her turbulent thoughts to give way to the blissful unconsciousness of sleep.

She needed her sleep. Tomorrow the adventure would begin. She hoped she was up to dealing with the job… and the man.

Chapter Four

Gideon stared at the towering mass of boxes in the ballroom the next day. He then looked at the slender woman standing before him. Okay, so maybe he *had* rushed into this a bit.

"So what do you think? Two, three assistants? An army? You're not feeling a bit like the miller's daughter who was asked to spin a roomful of straw into gold, are you?"

Caroline walked past him, her eyes aglow as if she'd just stepped into the perfect dream. "Are you kidding? This looks like fun. Just what *is* in all these boxes?"

Gideon crossed his arms and lounged against the door frame. "Who knows? Most of it was my mother's, and she kept almost everything. All the trappings of the main house were sent here while I was traveling. Except for the basics and my office equipment, I haven't opened any of it."

She wrinkled her nose at him. "You haven't even—

don't you have any sense of mystery, Gideon? There could be anything in those boxes. Treasure. Family history.''

''Possibly. My mother was into family history in a big way.'' And he had never been.

Caroline was almost dancing around, obviously imagining the possibilities. He couldn't help smiling, even though he really wasn't able to dredge up any enthusiasm over what she was likely to find. If his mother had kept mementos of the family's history, it hadn't been for sentimental reasons. Caring wasn't in her soul. She'd been a woman who kept her distance. As he did.

But the lady kneeling before him now *did* care about a great many things. And she was looking so darn eager. ''We'll look together,'' he said. ''I'll help you begin.'' Guilt over just how much work he was giving her seeped in.

''You don't have work to do?'' She turned from where she had started struggling to free a box from the stack.

There was a ton of work waiting for him. He hadn't been able to concentrate last night and hadn't gotten anything done.

''I'll help you, Caroline,'' he said again, nudging her aside and placing his hands on the box. His fingers touched hers and he ignored the intense jolt of sensation that winged its way through his body. He carefully set the box on the floor. ''As soon as possible, we'll find you some assistants,'' he said. And he would return to work, far away from her. He needed the distance *and* the distraction. Caroline had a right to know that she could trust him not to touch, or look at her with eyes that smoldered or even to think about laying his lips against hers.

She looked up into his eyes, visibly swallowing, then quickly knelt to begin opening the box. "You don't have to hire anyone," she protested. Her voice was low and soft, but he resisted the urge to move closer in order to hear better. "You're paying a lot of money for my help."

"I'll pay a little more to keep you from killing yourself out of a sense of responsibility."

A lilting laugh drifted to him. "You obviously don't have any idea how much energy I have, Gideon. But if it will make you feel better, hire away. Just let me spend a day or so getting organized. Even delegating chores takes planning."

"I believe you. You seem to be good at organizing," he said, as she leaned over the box. Her hair swayed forward, a bright curtain of silk that caught on her jeans and white blouse. She tossed it over her shoulder, an unconscious gesture she must have repeated a million times.

But not while he'd been there to appreciate the gentle twisting of her body, the way her hair had fallen back into a long, loose river of dark, silky stuff laced with red light. Not when he'd been envisioning that hair swaying over his bare chest as he reared up on his bed to kiss her lips.

Damn, but she was driving him insane with want already and she wasn't even casting out any lures. She was just unpacking boxes. And smiling over her shoulder at him. She held up a linen tablecloth, embroidered with the Tremayne crest.

"Pretty impressive. There must be a ton of these in here," she said, looking back inside.

"Probably." He stepped forward to move another box. "Don't even touch that. You can't lift this stuff alone."

She chuckled. "Tell my brother Darryl that I'm too delicate to do heavy labor, won't you? I used to pound on him regularly when we were young."

Gideon grinned at the picture she painted. "Well, since I'm assuming you didn't also pick him up and throw him on the ground, I'll take the liberty of providing you with someone for the heavy labor. Better for your back, Caroline." And if there were someone else here, the situation would be safer. He wouldn't be so distracted by whatever it was about her that was making him act as if he'd never spent a night in a woman's bed.

But Caroline had moved beyond the topic of assistants. He could tell by the rapturous look on her face. She was pulling things out of the second box, quickly assessing each item, and sorting. She looked efficient...and enchanting.

She paused suddenly in her search.

"Look Gideon, is this you?" She held up a photo for him to see. "And your mother?"

The color was slightly faded, but he didn't need to see the woman in the picture to know it wasn't his mother. The family pictures were all very formal. No smiling faces. They'd been taken for the purpose of documenting history and for no other reason. He and Erin had always hated those sessions. The two of them had hated the fact that their mother's obsession with the family's status had made her frown on many of their activities that other children considered normal.

"Not my mother, no. A nanny."

Caroline nodded. "She must have been close to you. She's smiling at you. What was her name?"

He reached for another box. "I don't remember."

The sudden silence was awkward and heavy. "You don't remember your nanny's name?"

He really didn't want to talk about this. "I had a number of them, Caroline. I think…maybe that one's name was Jane. I'm not sure."

"Why so many? Were you difficult?"

"Sometimes." But the real reason hadn't had anything to do with him. His father had tired of the hired help just as easily as he'd fallen into lust. There was no way Gideon was going to mention that. Or that the reason he couldn't remember the names of the women who cared for him was because he'd learned not to connect when goodbye was inevitable. Still, that was long ago, unimportant, and Caroline was waiting. He struggled to remember what he'd once labored to forget.

"Jane liked riddles," he recalled. "Bad ones. She had an infectious laugh, and she snitched oatmeal cookies from the kitchen for me sometimes."

"She liked you," Caroline said with a sigh and a smile, as though he'd righted the world with one simple memory. "I would hate to think that a child had been left in the care of a woman he couldn't even remember and who didn't do at least one memorable good thing. That wouldn't say anything good about her."

"Is that what you do with your students? Try to do something memorable for them?"

"I try. Not that it's a hardship. Kids are great. They're spontaneous and still willing to believe in things that adults have deemed impossible. I love teaching."

"It's a great responsibility. *Children* are a great responsibility."

She sat back on her knees. "I suppose they are, but you say that as if you're giving a lecture. Is that what one of your nannies told you?"

He shook his head and smiled. "It's just the truth."

But a frown now marred Caroline's smooth brow. "Your childhood—was it perhaps…difficult?"

He looked down at her, a woman who had told him she'd been raised in a big family with no money. A woman who had committed herself to teaching children despite the difficulties that might entail. And she had stood on the auction block yesterday not knowing what her fate would be, an act that most certainly would be frightening for most people—and difficult.

Gideon shook his head again. "No one has a perfect childhood, but I *was* raised in a privileged family with money and advantages other children don't often have. Because of that, I probably managed to get away with a lot of things most teenage boys never would. And while my parents weren't warm people, I wasn't alone. I had Erin. I've had a very pampered life, Caroline, so don't go getting that 'poor little rich kid' look on your face. It won't fly."

"Okay." She wrinkled her nose at him. "What kind of things did you get away with as a teenager? Were you very wicked?"

"Forget it, Caroline." He moved closer to lift the box she was attempting to move. "I'm not telling any secrets about my wild younger years to a teacher who'd probably just love to analyze and excuse my bad habits. Let's just say I had money and opportunity once I hit my teens, and that the combination can provide a young man with an interesting social life.''

She rose from the box she was examining and slapped dust off her hands. ''Women,'' she said decidedly, with a smile.

He smiled back. ''I didn't say that.''

''You didn't have to. Just look at you.''

''I'm looking at *you*,'' he mused. ''Did you have a lot more Bobby Cummingses in your life?''

Caroline planted her palms against her sides and applied pressure. There most certainly had been more boys like Bobby Cummings. Boys who looked at her body and tuned into her fun-loving manner and got the wrong idea. Or men who wanted to be seen with that wild O'Donald woman—for a while.

''I've certainly been involved since Bobby,'' she admitted, ''but as I said, I'm not looking for love or romance. I want a man who'll simply be a partner.''

''But you once wanted romance. You wanted Bobby Cummings badly,'' he reminded her, taking out his handkerchief and gently stroking it over a smudge on her cheek.

The warmth of his fingers filtered through. She looked up into his eyes and then wished she hadn't.

''A marriage of convenience can be cold,'' Gideon said. ''I know that. My parents married for duty, and most women I've known tell me they want the trimmings eventually, even if they're not in the market for marriage right now. They want to feel a glow about the man they marry. Wouldn't you miss that?''

Caroline swallowed. ''You mean the weak knees, the heart that plays hopscotch?'' The way hers was doing right now.

"Who needs those kinds of feelings?" she asked, moving away and reaching for another carton. She absolutely could not give in to that shaky, heart-fluttering kind of feeling again. And it wasn't that she didn't love roller-coaster rides. It was just that part of what she liked was knowing she would arrive safely.

"I just want a friend and a father for my children," she reiterated. "The basics. I'm a very simple lady."

Gideon lowered his hand to his side and looked over to where she had stepped several feet away from him.

"I'm beginning to think you're a very smart lady, Caroline," he said in that deep, cultured voice that made her want him to whisper something, anything, against her lips.

"You're very wise," he reiterated. "I'd like to think I am, too, so I'll just move some of these boxes out into the open for you, and then I think I'll hit the office the way any wise man should on a work day. Call me when you need me."

She nodded slowly, but when he'd finally left the room, she raised her hand to her cheek and stroked two fingers down the place where his own fingers had been just moments ago.

There was no way she was calling Gideon back into the room to move more boxes. In the last year, she'd decided she liked having her heartbeat moving along at a steady rate most of the time. Oh sure, she liked being in the thick of the action, maybe even being a bit daring now and then. She'd snuck into the drive-in with Albert Murray when she was still too young for her parents to give permission. She'd had her year of tight black leather skirts so short she'd been sent home from school three times. But even in her crazy younger days, she'd never been an idiot. She didn't jump off of cliffs onto the rocks—or dive into water wearing lead underwear. And she wouldn't get close to a man like Gideon Tremayne. He could break a woman's heart without even knowing it. No doubt he'd done that very thing to a thousand women. She was not going to be woman number one thousand and one.

So, for the rest of the day she wouldn't even be a woman, just the perfect employee. And no way would she leave here crying the way Paula Masters had.

"Caroline, I promise I wouldn't ask this of you if there was anyone else I could turn to, but you know how much I need this promotion, and you also know Libby doesn't sleep well when she stays with anyone but you. If you can't watch her for me for the next few weeks, I can't attend the training sessions, and if I don't attend the training, I—"

"Won't get this promotion. I understand that, Tracy," Caroline said to her younger sister later that evening. "I do, but hon, you know I'm not even home right now. And my employer, well, he wouldn't want a baby here, I'm afraid."

The silence on the other end of the line lasted a long time. Caroline could tell her sister was trying to get a grip on herself, and she longed to take back her words, to fly across town and hug Tracy close the way she had when they were small. Her sister's life had been anything but easy since she'd had to face life as a single mother.

"You know I'd do anything for you and Libby," Caroline reasoned.

"I know. I do." Tracy's voice was small and lost.

"They can't move the training to another time?"

"It's been scheduled for weeks. I was the last one chosen to go."

"And there won't be any other?"

"Maybe in another year or so."

But Tracy needed the promotion now. She needed the money, but more than that, she needed the self-confidence she'd lost to that jerk she'd been married to. And Caroline would do just about anything to try and repair the damage Guy had done.

"I could—maybe—Darryl," Tracy finally said, her voice growing more firm even as her words faltered.

But they both knew their brother's job took him out of the house for too long. They knew both of their sisters were touring Europe. Libby, still so little, would be frightened if she was left with sitters too, long, and frankly, Darryl didn't know beans about how to choose a good sitter.

"Not Darryl," Caroline said, holding back a sigh. "Me. And why not? Why shouldn't I take care of my niece? This is a big place, and I'm sure Gideon will understand. The man is, after all, donating a lot of money to a children's charity. Besides, who couldn't look at Libby and not love her on sight?"

But they both knew the answer to that. The child's father didn't love her. And in her line of work, Caroline frequently met people who didn't love their children.

"Send her, Trace. I'll make all the arrangements."

"Caroline, I wouldn't if…I mean, I hate asking you. I hate sending her away. I…"

"Trace, I love her. And you, too. I care."

"Me, too, Caroline. I love you both, and—thank you.

You're not to worry, either. She's so good, Mr. Tremayne won't even notice she's there.''

But as Caroline got off the phone after making arrangements to pick up Libby, she had to shake her head at the thought. Libby was a love, but she was a sweet, *noisy* love. And she was a baby. There was no way Gideon wasn't going to notice a baby living right here in his house.

She'd spent the day and half the evening attacking the mountain of work she had to do, clearing away, sorting, planning and trying not to panic at the thought that she might not be able to get everything done or carry off the business of being Gideon's refined hostess. As a result of her wild panic and hard work, she'd accomplished a great deal, but now there was this. So much for her plans to be the perfect employee. Just how was the man going to react to having a second—and unwelcome—visitor?

Gideon had his fingers poised over the keyboard when he heard the knock at his office door. For a full two seconds he hesitated. And it wasn't because he'd been working so hard. No, his hesitation stemmed from the fact that he needed a second to brace himself, to get ready for that white-hot jolt of want he knew he'd feel when he opened the door and looked into her eyes.

But she was waiting.

He opened the door. He looked. He beat back the heat with a great amount of effort.

"Caroline," he said softly. "You need something?"

"Yes, I—" She stared at him wide-eyed, biting on her lip slightly, the soft flesh yielding to small, white teeth.

Gideon concentrated on breathing normally.

"I—" She blew out a long breath of air. "I just—oh, what the heck, I'm absolutely not good at beating around the bush. I just wanted to tell you that you might want me to leave. Right away, too."

He raised his brows. "Because—"

Her brow furrowed and she clenched her hands. She paced across the room. "My sister has been unexpectedly called away from home. She needs me to care for my niece. Libby's just eighteen months old and my sister Tracy is divorced. Her ex-husband is not an option for childcare. I'm the only one available, and I said I'd do it, that she could bring Libby here, but—"

"But if I object, you're willing to leave," he said slowly, carefully.

"Yes. *Do* you object?"

She looked straight up into his eyes, her own clear, blue, and very deep. And achingly beautiful, Gideon couldn't help thinking.

So much for managing his breathing. But that didn't matter now, because, yes, he did object. His plan had seemed slightly out of the ordinary, a bit outrageous before, but now? How would Erin view the fact that his current "lady of the moment" was taking care of a baby? And besides, he knew nothing of children except that he didn't want to be around them. Babies were so fragile, so small—so in need of deep emotions, commitment, and inherent knowledge he didn't possess any more than his parents had. He'd once been left in charge of his cousins for a short time, and in that time one of them had been injured. And the son of that woman he'd dated—oh hell, that little boy had looked at him with big, accusing eyes every time Gideon had even entered the room. The memory had stayed with him for a long time afterwards. Did a man really want to risk going through that again? Putting a *kid* through that again? No, he did not.

Yet Caroline was looking up at him, still biting her lip. He wondered if she knew that when she was nervous her hands would not stay still. She was sliding them down her jeans right now.

He wanted to catch them in his own, still their movements, reassure her.

"I'd be lying if I said this was an easy question to answer, Caroline." Of course, the true answer was easy, but the one he would give was still up in the air.

"This wasn't what you'd planned. I understand." She rose to go. He held out one hand and almost touched her to hold her in place before he lowered his arm to his side.

"It isn't what I'd planned," he agreed. "But—"

"You'll feel uncomfortable with a baby around."

He'd feel worse than uncomfortable. He might not know what children were all about, but he knew that they had a right to expect to be left in the care of adults who could care and respond. And know what to do. He couldn't. That wasn't the way he was made. But this child wouldn't really be in his care. She'd just be a guest, one he wouldn't even have to interact with. And she would be very temporary. Not a real commitment.

"I'll find someone else for you," Caroline volunteered.

She would, but he didn't want someone else. He had the feeling there weren't many women like Caroline around. Not many who would look at a roomful of clutter and work and think of it as an adventure. Not many who would have her grit and determination, or who could soothe Erin's fears with a smile the way he thought this woman might be able to.

"How will you manage a baby and a job?" he asked, and this time he allowed himself to touch her. He cradled her shoulders in his palms and turned her to face him.

"I always manage almost everything I set out to do," she said softly. "Libby won't be a problem for me. But for you?"

He took a long breath, even managed a hint of a smile. "I'm running out of time, Caroline, and if I asked Mrs. Williams to help me, well, somehow I just don't think that entertaining is her hobby of choice. Or that Erin would go away convinced that I was in good hands."

"But then again, entertaining might be Mrs. William's secret passion," Caroline said, smiling back at him. "Gideon, Libby won't—"

"I was hiring help for you, anyway," he reasoned, "and it's not as if you're asking *me* to take care of a baby. This is just a place for her to stay. It's a big house and an eighteen-month-old child is pretty small. Your niece is your niece forever, after all, but this job is only for a few weeks. So if you're sure you can manage..."

"Trust me, Gideon. I'll manage to do it all. And thank you." She laid her hand on his cheek in an age-old gesture of reassurance, then froze as her skin connected, the soft tips of her fingers sliding against the rough edges of his face. He could almost feel her quick intake of breath as she stepped away. She flashed him a quick smile and turned to go.

But the memory of her fingers feathering over him lingered. He closed his eyes, searching for some other sensation to chase away the burn of her touch.

As he closed the door, he decided that it was probably

not such a bad thing that the child was coming, after all. Caroline's hours would be full, and he wouldn't be able to get too close to those tempting, fluttering hands if she had them filled with boxes and babies.

Okay, she was finding it difficult to sleep tonight, Caroline admitted, slipping into her robe. She'd been trying to relax for what seemed like a millennium, but she just couldn't do it. Even her favorite hobby, writing, hadn't helped as it usually did. The problem, of course, was the man down the hall.

"You'd think a woman could just ignore a man in a place this big," she muttered. Especially given the fact that she'd barely seen him since early this evening. He'd stayed in his office. She'd stayed at her job, and her room—well, she'd taken his good advice and moved herself far away from him.

But her thoughts kept creeping down the hall. She couldn't help wondering about Gideon. He didn't want kids, and yet he'd been kind in letting her force Libby on him. She shouldn't have done that. Everyone knew Gideon could have a new woman here in a heartbeat. The man was the type to attract beautiful women. He probably slayed them with that sexy grin and that voice that made a woman feel like she'd die if he didn't touch her soon. So she should have resigned and found him a more sophisticated replacement, someone capable of impressing his sister.

Besides, the man made her nervous. He made her want just by opening those deep gray eyes, which was just crazy. She had a plan for her life, a good plan to fulfill her dreams and make a family, and darn it, it was made of stone. There was no part of the deal that said she could detour and risk falling for a man who was totally out of reach, didn't do forever or families, and who could break her heart like a breadstick.

"Dumb, dumb, dumb, Caroline," she said. "You had the perfect opportunity to bow out." But if he hired someone from an agency, Summerstaff would have to repay the money.

"So I stay. That's it." She would just watch herself. Every second. Because thinking about what it would be like to feel Gideon's lips against hers was not a smart move. The only man she should even think about kissing was the unknown man she meant to marry.

Besides, no matter how kind the man had been about Libby, that didn't mean he wasn't dangerous. Paula Masters had cried when she'd left here. Noisily. She'd shed tears at the Laundro-Clean, the Starshine Tavern, and had told everyone in her step aerobics class that she'd fallen for Gideon and been cut loose. Word had traveled along the active Eldora grapevine.

"But I'm not Paula." Caroline yanked a brush through her hair, happily noting that her eyes looked cool and clear in the mirror, not dreamy at all. "And I'm not going to be a prisoner to my urges," she said with great determination. "At least not to any but the safe ones. Like…late-night urges for ice cream." The inspiration filled her with relief. At last she'd found a workable distraction and an innocent path for her thoughts.

"Okay. Ice cream, then. Let's see just what Gideon has tucked into his freezer."

But to do that, she would have to go downstairs, moving right past his door. And maybe that was half the reason she was going. She had never allowed herself to be a true victim for long, not even of her own thoughts. It just wasn't going to start happening now.

Besides, there was nothing like a big scoop of the good stuff to restore a woman's mood. So, pulling the belt on her white chenille robe tight, Caroline headed for the kitchen and the promise of forbidden frozen delights.

Once downstairs and inside the massive black and white and chrome kitchen, she located the freezer, lifted the lid, and peered inside.

"Hmm…"

She moved a few packages around, looking for treasure.

Nothing.

She dug deeper. And deeper. In a few minutes she had completely rearranged the contents.

Caroline wrinkled her nose. "No ice cream? What kind of person doesn't keep ice cream around? Yeah, like I don't know the answer to that. A deprived person, that's what kind. A man who hires a cook who can't cook. A poor, clueless man who probably knows more about the social register or how to unfasten a woman's buttons than what's inside the walls of a grocery store," she continued muttering, leaning way over into the freezer, her bare toes just touching the floor as she pushed through all the frozen packages. She dug to the bottom again just in case she'd missed something.

"Rats. There's none here at all."

She placed her hands on the edge of the freezer and pushed off, lowering the freezer lid. "Darn."

"Something wrong, Caroline?"

That deep, low voice came from behind her and across the width of the room. She barely stopped herself from screeching. Instead she turned, looking at the man who stood leaning against the wall, his arms crossed as he studied her. He was wearing a pair of black silk pajama bottoms and nothing else. His hair was mussed, his naked shoulders were magnificent, but it was that wicked raised eyebrow that told her he'd caught her doing something he considered a bit odd.

"No, of course not. I…was just looking for a midnight snack, Gideon."

One corner of his lips quirked up. "You were talking."

She shrugged sheepishly and smiled. "Oh that. I always do that. I was raised with a brother and three sisters. Someone was *always* talking. Now when I'm alone, I tend to talk just to hear the sound of someone's voice."

"And you were saying…" He uncrossed his arms and moved away from the wall, closer to her.

What had she been saying? Caroline's mind raced, moving backward a few paces. Uh-oh, what *had* she been saying? Had she actually called the man clueless and deprived? Had she talked about him unfastening a woman's buttons?

She held out her hands and stepped away from the freezer.

"Nothing important. Really."

She thought he'd pursue the topic. She had, after all, called him names and commented on his sex life, but he simply nodded and kept walking toward her.

"If there's something you want, Caroline, all you have to do is ask." His voice was soft, a bare whisper, and he was still moving her way.

She opened her mouth to answer, but she, who never had trouble with words, suddenly couldn't find any. She wanted…oh, what did she want? She wanted to hear that voice, even softer, his lips at her ear, his breath warming hers, his hands....

"Ice cream," she suddenly blurted out, when he was only steps away. "You don't—"

She took a long, deep breath, calming her voice. "You don't have any ice cream."

"And that upsets you?"

"Yes. I mean no." She realized she was clutching the low neckline of her robe closed. "That is, of course it isn't really upsetting, Gideon," she said, finally gaining control of herself. "But it's just something that most people keep around. I have to say, you don't look like you're a man who needs to watch his weight, but you eat bland food, whatever your cook puts in front of you, apparently. Don't you have any preferences, any weaknesses, any...cravings?"

"For—?" He was staring at her lips, his eyelids half closed.

She shook her head. "Never mind. It doesn't really matter, anyway."

Inhaling deeply, she tried to smile, intending to pull away.

But he held out one hand, placed it on her arm. A gentle grip. No pressure. She could feel the heat of him through the thick chenille and for a second she wished there was nothing separating her skin from his. Struggling to still her shuddering breath, swaying slightly, she looked up into his eyes.

For a second he moved close. The tang of his after-shave, the soap-clean scent of him filled her senses, making her dizzy. He tilted his head, tucked one finger beneath her chin.

And then he stopped dead. The sound of the refrigerator humming seemed to fill the room. Guilt and regret and something that almost looked like anger flared in Gideon's gray eyes. He carefully unfurled his fingers from her sleeve and relinquished physical contact.

He cleared his throat.

"Cravings?" he said softly, as though their conversation had never stopped. "I'm afraid I've never paid much attention to what goes on in the kitchen, Caroline. I hire someone and she takes care of the food while I take care of my business. But if it's ice cream you want, feel free to let Mrs. Williams know."

She wanted to clear her throat herself, or drink in great gulps of air, but she took her cue from his tone. Keep things light. Get back on the right path.

And so she tilted her head. "Maybe...yes, I think I will get to know the lady better. I'm sure she'll be understanding and kind once we've discussed the matter. Before I leave here, you'll have something more interesting to eat. Don't worry."

"I'm not worried."

"You should be," she said, trying to hold a smile and to ignore the beautiful bare expanse of his chest right in front of her eyes. "Gideon, how can you make midnight forays to the freezer without a half gallon of the good stuff there waiting for you?"

"The good stuff?"

She smiled in earnest then, relaxing a bit.

"Top-quality ice cream. I'll get you some. See to it personally, and you'll see what I mean. What flavor do you like?"

He looked at her as if she'd gone mad. "Vanilla?"

Caroline frowned and concentrated on maintaining her

breezy course. "Vanilla. No rocky road? No double-chocolate cherry?"

Gideon's brows raised. She could see these were foreign substances to him.

"Okay," she said with a sigh. "Vanilla, but only the good kind. And maybe something a bit more exotic, too. I'll bring you some samples. You don't mind trying new things, do you?"

"I *am* trying new things," he said with the burgeoning hint of a more relaxed smile. "You're different from anyone I've ever known, Caroline, so let's just say that I'm trying you."

"Yes. Well." She swallowed hard at the vestige of heat in his eyes. "I suppose that's true. And I've been told I'm a handful, so I guess you really are on shaky ground here." She opened her mouth to continue on, knowing she was starting to babble, but she just couldn't help it. The longer they stood there, the more aware she became of the fact that she was wearing very little beneath her robe and he, well, he was wearing very little, period. Maybe if she just kept talking, she might not think—or want. He might not be able to think, either.

"Gideon, I—"

He held up one hand, placed it over her lips to close them, then quickly pulled away as if he couldn't bear to touch her for very long.

"Don't," he said simply. "Don't. It's only for three weeks. Surely we can survive without me touching you. Because, despite what people think, I don't…do this with my employees, Caroline. It would be taking advantage of my position. And once you leave here, well, we both know our chosen paths don't intersect. You're not a woman for a brief affair, and I'm not a man meant for marriage. So I'm doing my best to do the right thing and keep my hands to myself.''

He was. She could see by the hard line of his jaw and his clenched fists that he was holding himself in check.

She should be grateful, she thought, as he moved away and left the room. She *was* grateful. They would both survive this temporary temptation. There was nothing at all to worry about.

Except that she was going to have to deal with the terrible, awful fact that she really had wanted to feel Gideon's lips against hers. And heaven help her, she still did.

Chapter Five

The little girl arrived two days after his midnight meeting with Caroline, just two hours after Roy, a local college student, had taken up his post as Caroline's muscleman. Gideon knew exactly when Libby had arrived even though he wasn't there in person to greet the lady's niece. He knew it because, after the doorbell rang, there was a sudden change in the noise level of his house. Not that things became noticeably louder the way he'd expected them to, but because the house fell silent. Tiptoe silent.

''So how do you feel now that you've got the lady whispering, trying not to disturb you?'' he asked himself.

Like a tyrant, was the answer, although the thought of Caroline working so hard to restrain herself brought a smile to his face. This was a woman who talked to herself when there was no one else to listen. Not talking at all when there was an audience would probably entail a huge effort. But she was doing it because she thought it was what he wanted. And while he wasn't sure what he *did* want, he knew he didn't want his employees fussing for his sake. That road smacked of his father's autocratic ways.

So Gideon pushed back from his desk, and marched off in search of Caroline.

Shoving open his office door, he made his way down the hall. The ballroom was empty. The door to the library was closed.

Gideon knocked and then swung the door back. Three sets of startled eyes greeted him. He briefly registered a young man effortlessly holding a heavy box in his arms. Roy of the sculpted muscles and the lifeguard good looks, Gideon noted.

''Nice to meet you, Roy,'' he said, holding out his hand. ''I'm Gideon Tremayne. My apologies for being in the middle of something when you arrived, but I'm glad to see you're already proving a help to Caroline.''

Roy set the box down and grinned broadly. ''Don't worry, Mr. Tremayne, I'll take good care of your woman. Won't let her hurt that pretty little back of hers.'' The young man eyed Caroline with worshipful eyes. As if she were a dish of ice cream he coveted and which he had been commissioned to keep from melting.

Gideon raised one brow, turning to Caroline who had frozen at Roy's words. Her cheeks were faintly pink. She was trapped by the small chubby arms hugging her legs. Her hand was resting on the child's golden curls, protectively.

The baby looked up at Gideon, and began to whimper. He nearly took a step back, then stopped himself.

''Caroline, could I please speak to you in my office?''

Her color high, she nodded, bent down and began to whisper to the child as if explaining that she had to leave. The little girl stared back with wide blue eyes. She planted her tiny hands, stubby fingers splayed, on Caroline's cheeks. Puckering her lips, she gave her aunt a kiss, gurgling happily and lifting her arms to be held. Gideon stood transfixed, watching them charm each other, as Caroline picked up the baby and planted her on her hip. She turned to Gideon, a look of apology on her face, as she opened her mouth.

"No hurry, Caroline," he said quietly. "When you have time." And he returned to his office.

But he was barely seated when she appeared.

"You're alone," he said quietly, the question in his voice.

"Roy," she said with a grin. "He has several sisters who have babies. He's a love."

He quirked up one corner of his mouth. "You know that already, do you? The young man's only been here two hours."

She shrugged. "When the agency called to see if he'd arrived, I took the liberty of asking a number of questions. I figured there'd be a chance he would be left alone now and then with—well, I just wanted to make sure he was dependable."

He nodded, studying the way she was fiddling with the button on her shirt. The one lying directly between the soft curve of her breasts, he noted. That thought dropped in from nowhere, nailing him like a velvet baseball bat, but he sucked in a breath, and pushed onward.

He'd told her that he didn't get involved with his employees, but that wasn't the only reason he wouldn't allow himself to touch her. She was, after all, only working here for a short while, and she wasn't really dependent on him—for anything. But there was an innocence about her. She wanted a marriage and children—things that gave him chills and that he was completely incapable of wanting. He liked his relationships with women to be clean-edged and quick, but any man who offered Caroline clean-edged and quick deserved some serious pain, in Gideon's opinion.

He stood up straighter to clear his mind.

"Good, well I'm glad you asked about Roy. So you're satisfied with his help so far?"

"He's very...willing."

He smiled at her diplomacy. "And it doesn't bother you that he already has a crush on you?"

"Oh, that," she said, smiling and waving her hand in dismissal. "It's nothing. He's young."

Gideon leaned back against his desk, crossing his arms and ankles. "Twenty-one, according to the agency. A man, Caroline, with a man's desires."

She shook her head. "Believe me, Gideon, I can handle Roy. In a day or two, the new will wear off me, and he'll be on to someone else."

She said that as if she had men falling all over her and then walking away on a regular basis.

"Besides," she said, looking to the side, "he seems to think you and I—well, I just know Roy's not going to be a problem in that area."

Immediately Gideon remembered the young man's words. Roy thought that Gideon had staked a claim on Caroline.

Well, let him think that, then, Gideon told himself, even if it wasn't true. It was bad enough that he himself did a long, sustained burn every time he looked into the woman's eyes, or let his gaze rest on the fullness of her lips. Bad enough that he wanted to dip down and taste the curve of her jaw every time she pushed her hair back. He didn't want some other man doing the same, especially not some neophyte male who hadn't yet learned the tricks of controlling his most basic urges.

"Is he…being useful?"

She raised her lips in a deadly slow grin. "I can't even pick up a piece of paper without asking his permission, Gideon."

No question. The young guy had it bad.

"That's very good, then," Gideon agreed, studying Caroline's amused expression. No signs of infatuation on the lady's part. "But actually Roy isn't why I called you in here."

She opened her eyes wide and stood there staring at him for a few seconds. Then she took a deep breath.

"It's Libby."

He tilted his head. "You've gone to great lengths to make sure she doesn't disturb me in any way."

"But it's not working, is it?"

She sounded so resigned, he had the greatest urge to go to her and take her into his arms and offer comfort.

"Caroline, you can't knock yourself out hiding a baby."

"I know. That's not at all what you hired me to do."

"That's not what I meant."

She had lowered her head, but his words brought her chin up. He looked dead into those deep blue eyes and plunged on.

"Just because I choose not to be a father, Caroline, it doesn't mean I'd ask you to hide a child as if she were a sinful secret. Maybe this wasn't the arrangement I had in mind when I hired you, but surely I can survive whatever noise an eighteen-month-old girl can make. How loud can she be?''

Caroline just looked at him and shook her head, a growing smile on her face. ''I know you're not heartless, but did you say you were clueless, Gideon?''

''Let's give it a try,'' he suggested. ''I'm in my office a great deal, anyway. You don't have to padlock yourself and—''

''And Libby,'' she prompted.

''Of course,'' he agreed, with a long nod. ''You don't have to barricade yourself and the baby in a room for my sake.'' Especially not with Roy on the wrong side of the door, he thought.

She and Roy had gotten a lot accomplished, Caroline mused late that afternoon, as she emptied the last box for the day and set it aside, but there was still so much to be done. Gideon's mother *had* saved everything just as he'd said. So far, Caroline had uncovered gorgeous vases, jewel boxes and crystal. She'd also found tiny scraps of lace and silk, meaningless newspaper clippings and lots of empty perfume bottles. Still, order was arising from the chaos. Maybe tomorrow she could take some of the covers off the furniture and hang some family portraits.

The ringing of the household phone line clipped off her thoughts. She grabbed it before it could transfer into Gideon's office, and by the time Caroline had hung up the line, she was making a mad dash for the sound of Roy's receding footsteps.

''Roy, you got a minute?''

The young man turned, a look of pure pleasure and anticipation on his face.

Caroline blew out a sigh. The young ones were so easy. Probably because they didn't bother thinking about their tomorrows, she reasoned. And right now she shouldn't be either. There was still a fair amount of today remaining.

''Roy, if you have some free time—''

''Anything you want, Caroline.''

She barely stifled a smile. ''Well, good then, since I need someone to watch Libby for me. Mrs. Williams called in sick and I need to run to the grocery store. I'll pay you overtime,'' she added. ''Double whatever Gideon is paying you.''

He barely lost a beat in switching the directions of his thoughts. An indignant frown creased his young, handsome face. ''Extra money? For taking care of the little squirt? No way, Caroline. She and I are buddies. This one's on me.''

Caroline wanted to hug him. ''Roy, you're an angel. Top of the list of the good guys. Thanks. I owe you. Remember.''

''I will,'' he said with a teasing smile. ''Next time I need to make some girl jealous, I'll be counting on you to put on an act for me.''

''Hey, no sweat. What are friends for?'' she agreed as she turned toward the hall on her way to Gideon's office.

She knocked on the door and waited. When Gideon answered, Caroline took one look at that wickedly handsome face and everything practical fled her body. The man just made her feel reckless. She scrambled for coherent thought.

"Gideon, I...something's come up and I have to leave."

He frowned, his dark brows nearly meeting. "You're leaving? Caroline, what's this all about? If that puppy has—"

She held up one hand. "Mrs. Williams isn't coming. You need to be fed and so I'm going to the store."

She thought he'd stop frowning, but she was wrong.

"You're going shopping for my dinner?"

"Yes, well, I've already gone shopping for you. I slipped out yesterday and bought ice cream," she reminded him. She'd run into her friend Rebecca, and later they'd met Emily and Emily's employer for the summer, Simon.

Gideon tilted his head. "I know you did, just as you said you would. But this is different. I didn't hire you to cook."

"Do *you* want to cook?"

He grinned. "You'd be sorry."

She grinned back. "I'm sure I would be."

"We'll eat out."

"Not with Libby here. I've done restaurants with her, thank you very much. She's a love, but she's at that age when she likes to squeal. Restaurant patrons generally like a bit of quiet with their meal."

He didn't answer.

Probably didn't want to even think of the vision she had called up, she thought.

"Gideon, you hired me to take charge of your household. That's what I'm doing."

"Yes, but cooking wasn't on the agenda."

"I don't know what will be on the agenda once Erin and her guests arrive. Neither do you. I need to learn how to handle anything.'' She tried not to imagine herself attempting to feel at ease with a group of born-to-wealth-and-power women. Panic threatened to rise like overactive bread dough every time she realized Gideon's sister would be here in just two weeks. Failing Gideon, when he seemed to have so much faith in her, just wasn't an option to consider.

''Tonight, I'm cooking,'' she said, starting toward the door. ''Things might be a little later than usual.''

But he had already anticipated her move. He stepped around her.

''If you insist on being stubborn, and I can see that you do,'' he said with a trace of amusement in his voice, ''then I'll drive you.'' He looked down at her, a solid male barrier between her and the door.

''Gideon, you don't have to come. I just need—''

''I'll drive you, Caroline,'' he said slowly. Insistently. ''If you're going to go above and beyond and cook for me, the least I can do is lend a hand.''

And that was how she found herself in the produce section of the grocery store with the grandson of a knight. She'd never seen so many eyes turning her way since the day she accidentally knocked a half-dozen rutabagas onto the floor. Not that she could blame anyone for looking at the man. Gideon made a tasty addition to the rows of green peppers and summer squash. His tall, lean frame and Heathcliff-like, dark good looks were no doubt a treat for those women shopping for dinner after a long day at the office.

''What can I do for you?'' he asked, and she had to remind herself that he was only talking about fruits and vegetables.

"A lemon," she told him, smiling at her own foolishness.

"Lemon," he repeated. "And those would be…"

"The yellow ones," she prompted.

His laugh was low and sexy. "I'm vaguely aware of what a lemon is, Caroline. I merely wanted you to point me in the right direction."

His comment and his laugh shattered her discomfort, enough for her to appreciate how awkward he must have felt when Dina, who managed the produce department, elected to give him a few samples of her section's wares a few minutes later.

"Have a passion fruit, Mr. Tremayne," she offered. "And a casaba melon. Very ripe. Very juicy. Very—"

"I think I've got everything here, Gideon. Thanks so much, Dina." Caroline said, tugging on his arm as she steered him toward the back of the store.

"You didn't have to take it," she muttered, as he held out the melon.

"I wasn't sure. Is there, after all, a polite way to turn down a casaba melon?" he asked, and she saw that his eyes were twinkling when she looked his way.

"I'm not sure, especially when it's a ripe, juicy one, but 'no thanks' might have done it. It usually works for me," she explained. "But, still, thank you for not making Dina feel silly or hurt. She works hard, and I get the feeling she doesn't have a lot of pleasure in her life."

He stared at her. Intensely. As if he were trying to figure out a puzzle. Those dangerous, dark eyes of his gazed into her own, and the store seemed to fade into the background. She was on the verge of swaying into him when he reached out to take the grocery list from her.

"Maybe we should go our separate ways and meet back at the front of the store," he suggested.

Caroline nodded, glad for the opportunity to be clear of his hot eyes and those wonderful hands with the long, strong fingers that she kept wanting to feel on her skin.

"Good heavens, O'Donald, get a connection to reality here, will you?" She scolded herself. She tried to clear her mind, to concentrate on the task at hand and forget the man she was here with.

When she finally reconnected with him, he had a cart full of things that she hadn't put on the list. She raised her brows and gave him a knowing look.

"More Dinas?" she guessed. "You're not even going to be hungry enough to eat later. I saw you at the deli counter. The clerk was giving you samples of everything but her neck."

He studied a flyer he'd picked up somewhere. "She offered that, too, but I resisted. And no, I'm the guilty party who picked up most of this. Do you realize that there are twelve kinds of olives on the shelves?"

She couldn't keep from smiling. "We have to get you out of that office more often, Gideon. You definitely spend too much time with your computers. Come on, let's go home and cook. And later," she said, "I'll show you what heaven is really like."

Silence. "I thought we weren't going to do that."

She put one hand to her cheek to make sure it wasn't turning hot.

"I meant the ice cream, Gideon. Mrs. Williams was very upset with me for taking over a corner of her freezer, but of course, after I bribed her with a big scoop of Peppermint Passion, she was a changed woman. My slave. Still, I don't know what she's going to say to all *this,*" she said, pointing to their very full cart.

"We'll bribe her some more," Gideon offered.

"With ice cream?"

"And olives," he promised.

She couldn't hold back her answering grin. This was a man who held the world in his hands. He had money, property, a business he obviously found fascinating and women when he wanted them. He had a sister who adored him, a house to die for. But, Caroline suspected, he'd missed out on a few things in life. Twelve kinds of olives. Imagine that.

She was a human tornado in the kitchen, Gideon concluded later, watching her attack a pile of vegetables with a knife.

"You might not want to witness this process," she warned. "I am definitely not a sane or neat woman while I'm cooking."

That was a delightful bit of understatement, Gideon thought with amusement as he watched her scrape the vegetables from the chopping board into a pan, and shut a cabinet with a delicious thrust of one of her lovely hips at the same time. She was all storm and clatter and scrumptious, mind-shattering movement, but the very intensity with which she approached the task turned his guilt button on. If his cook was ill, it was not this lady's duty to stand in as substitute.

"Caroline," he said, touching the soft skin of her arm, snagging her attention. "Let me lend you a hand."

"You want to help?"

What he wanted was to swoop her into his arms and calm her, to assure her that this really wasn't that important. It was just a meal and he had enjoyed plenty of meals, good and bad. Food wasn't that big a deal to him.

But when he moved closer, she gave him a quick, panicked look, and he remembered the last time they'd been in this kitchen alone and the risks involved.

"You need food, Gideon. So do I. But really, I'll be much more comfortable if you just let me go to it. My business as a teacher is, after all, very preparation-oriented."

As he was clearly making her life more difficult by being here, he bowed out, retired to the dining room to hunt out silver, dinnerware, linens, and candles.

When Caroline finally emerged from the kitchen with the dinner, it was already seven o'clock. She took one look at the white and burgundy linen, breathed in the faint scent of freesia, studied the crystal wineglasses.

"You certainly know what you're doing," she said.

He took the serving dishes from her. "My business as a computer consultant is, after all, very presentation-oriented."

"Then this works out very well," she conceded.

It certainly did. The red and green vegetables were lightly flavored with thyme, the delicately browned lemon chicken and rice could make a man cry with joy.

"It's wonderful," he told her. "Sinfully so."

She looked up, clearly startled, right into his eyes, then blushed. "Thank you, but this is just the beginning, Gideon."

He understood what she meant when, after the meal was over, she asked him to stay put while she left the room. When she returned, she was juggling a tray full of small containers of ice cream, and she had a black silk scarf in her hands.

"Now we find out what you like," she said with an elfin grin. "Sit back and let me blindfold you."

He raised one brow. "There's a reason for this?"

"Of course. I don't want you to be influenced by packaging or smooth names. This is supposed to be fun, Gideon. An ice cream adventure for those whose lives have been deprived of everything but vanilla."

"I've had chocolate," he offered.

She shook her head. "Doesn't count."

"Strawberry?"

"Only a few extra points. All right?" she asked, holding up the blindfold.

He leaned forward to allow her easier access. "Who am I to argue with the lady who made my taste buds sing at dinner."

She raised one brow. "It was only chicken, Gideon."

"Tell that to Mrs. Williams."

Her smile disappeared. "Don't."

"I won't," he promised softly, knowing what a soft spot this lady had for those who needed her help—for cooks and babies and overworked grocery produce managers. And, yes, even for wealthy but clueless businessmen. "I wouldn't hurt her, Caroline, and as I've said before, Mrs. Williams and I have a pact. She completes her part of it."

Then Caroline leaned forward into him, warm and lemon-scented, and she tied the soft silk around his eyes.

"Open," she said in that quiet, husky voice of hers. And she nudged his lips gently with the spoon.

He opened—and tasted cold, sweet, peaches and cream. His lips curved upward.

Her soft laughter caressed his senses as he savored, swallowed, and cleared his taste buds.

"Now this," she said, offering him a wickedly small taste of intense chocolate laced with—something.

"More?" she asked, and he could hear the smile in her voice. He felt her shift in front of him. Automatically his hands reached out to steady her. And so he was smoothing his palms over her waist when she offered him the bite of smooth, cool mint. The contrast of her warm body and the coolness of the ice cream hit him. He felt her tremble slightly as his hands tightened over her curves.

"Gideon?"

The broken whisper ripped right through him and the fragile web of control he'd been weaving for days shredded. Clasping her hips in his hands, he pulled her down onto his lap. He found her lips with his own. The coolness of his mouth met the warmth of her lips and he groaned, angling her closer as her fingers slid up into his hair.

"More," he whispered, when he broke off the kiss for air.

And then she was kissing him back, clutching at his shoulders, climbing into him.

His mind was a tangle of sensations. She was silk and heat and softness. He was hard and pulsing and damn near at the uncontrollable stage.

"Gideon," she said, and then kissed him again.

"Yes," he answered, and stroked his hands down her back and around to cup her breasts in his palms.

A soft gasp escaped her. She arched and moved closer. He groaned as the heat and his need rose higher. Consciousness began to recede and only a deep pulsing want remained.

And then she turned to cold stone in his hands. She freed her lips from his.

"Caroline." He ripped the blindfold from his eyes and rose with her still in his arms, but she was already pulling away.

"The baby" was all she said. Then he went cold as well. He had forgotten who he was, who she was, what they were doing here together in this house.

"Libby's awake," she said by way of explanation as she moved away from him. "I can feel it. I have to go to her."

For two seconds they stood there staring at each other, he by the table, she at the door.

Then he nodded. He had no business being here with her or thinking any of the things he'd been thinking.

"I'll see to the kitchen," he said simply. "Go. And Caroline?"

She turned to look at him.

"Thank you for dinner and...I apologize for crossing a line that should never have been crossed. We'll call it a night."

She stared at him, her eyes too wide for half a second. But then she nodded, one quick jerk of her head as she fled.

Chapter Six

Okay, so the man had kissed her and made her forget she even had a brain, that she was more than an aching body with needs too long unfulfilled. They'd practically burned down the dining room with that kiss. And it had been the dumbest thing she'd ever done in her life to melt down like that. No way should she have moved into that kiss when there was nothing there for her but a fast-burning relationship that would leave her singed and alone and still way shy of her goal of a family. There was no excuse for her actions even if she could still remember the feel of his mouth claiming hers three days after they'd touched.

Still, that didn't mean she could keep avoiding him, Caroline thought, as the late afternoon sunlight began to fade, and she frantically polished the woodwork in the morning room. Time was speeding by. They had yet to discuss the exact nature of her duties when his sister arrived, but for the last few days she'd been beating

herself up so badly she hadn't been able to do much
more than stumble over words in his presence.

"If the man didn't have millions already, he could
sell kisses and make another darn fortune," she muttered, attacking an antique rosewood table with her cloth.
Any woman would pay to have that skillful mouth on
any part of her body.

Except she wouldn't be one of those women. Gideon
had made it clear that he didn't kiss his employees and,
given the fact that he was right about the potential for
disaster between them, she ought to be ecstatic. She
didn't want to fall for a man like him. She wanted a
husband. She needed children. She was glad Gideon
wasn't interested in starting anything with her.

Or she would be, if it weren't for the way that he'd
said those words, "despite what everyone thinks, I don't
do this with my employees." People believed he had
wronged Paula Masters, but the force of Gideon's words
told her it just wasn't true.

"And what do you do? The man kisses you, apolo-
gizes, and you go around acting like you're afraid he's
going to attack you, when you know darn well he isn't
going to do any such thing. You're the one fighting the
urge to taste him again."

Caroline looked at her cloth. She'd been rubbing the
same spot on the table for the last two minutes. If she
didn't get things back on track with Gideon, she'd never
be ready by the time Erin arrived. Surely she was capable of controlling herself. Obviously Gideon was. For
the last few days he'd been courteous, but nothing more.
He probably assumed she believed the Paula Master's
heartbreak story, and he wouldn't deny it again. If she

wanted things back on the easy footing they'd started out on, it was up to her to take a step.

"Okay, O'Donald, time to stop running."

She dropped her cloth, and a few minutes later, knocked on Gideon's office door.

When he was home, he'd closed himself up in that gray and white cave for hours. Business, apparently, was Gideon's life.

When he came to the door, his dark hair was disheveled as if he'd been running his fingers through it. His tie hung loose where it had been yanked aside, his white shirt lay open at the collar, his sleeves were rolled to the elbows. He looked like a man who had been thoroughly explored by a woman. He made her very fingertips itch to touch.

Caroline dodged that thought, pasted on a smile and stood her ground.

"Have a tough day?" she asked, aiming for lightness.

"Had," he said simply. "I've just now convinced one of my clients to get rid of his antiquated computer system and swim with the big guys."

"Looks like it was quite a battle," she said with a grin and a nod to his less than pristine appearance.

"Took days to arm wrestle him to the floor."

She shook her head. "I don't understand. You're well-off. Why work so hard to make a sale?"

His grin finally came through. The man looked wonderful, even though the slight shadows beneath his eyes indicated some obvious late nights.

He held out his hands. "Ned and I go way back. He has several small stores in the state. One of them is in range of my Champaign office, so we've known each other awhile. I put in his original system. I couldn't let him get run over by the competition because he couldn't keep up. His old system was starting to create problems for him.''

Affection for the man he spoke of colored his voice. Caroline tried not to react to the warmth she heard there.

''So this is a good day?'' she asked. ''A day for a celebration, perhaps?''

A wary look came into his eyes. She remembered the last time they'd been together, she'd all but climbed into his bed.

''A very small celebration,'' she amended. ''I have things I need to discuss with you regarding your sister's visit, and it's getting close to dinner time. You look like you need to dig your way out of this office and get some air.''

She was pretty sure some of the reason he'd been locked in his office was because he felt guilty for touching her. He was, after all, a man who felt responsible— for his clients and his employees. She needed to show him she wasn't damaged, but in the open air, where temptation wouldn't follow her.

''Libby and I could use a small picnic, too,'' she added. ''An hour to eat and regroup before I tackle the morning room again.''

And that was all she needed to say.

''All right, a picnic, Caroline.'' He answered in that low voice that drove her wild with the need to get close.

She smiled and stepped back a bit just to be safe. In case she did something crazy, like deciding to jump Gideon.

''I'll have Mrs. Williams pack some sandwiches. Something simple and nonpoisonous,'' she promised.

He chuckled. "She'll probably feed us rocks to make us pay for changing her plans at this late date."

"I'll just tell her that tomorrow we'll eat what she's made for today and that way she can have an evening off."

"Clever lady. She probably deserves a day off, anyway. Have to see about giving her more paid vacation days even if it means eating takeout."

Caroline smiled at his wistful tone. Greasy burgers must seem like a treat compared to a steady diet of pureed peas and carrots. "Mrs. Williams adores you, anyway. You can do no wrong in her book."

"And in yours, Caroline O'Donald?"

"Well, you obviously care about your clients even when it means extra work for you. You must be a good guy."

He opened his mouth, probably to object, she surmised, and she quickly turned her back on him.

"Come on. The lake might dry up by the time we get there."

His chuckle was low and deep and seeped right through her bones to make her ache. She marched off to ask Mrs. Williams for a picnic basket and a tablecloth. A big tablecloth so that if Gideon laughed or smiled, she would be sitting too far away to crawl onto his lap and lift her lips to be kissed.

Gideon sat in the fading sunlight and breathed in deeply. The food had been edible, the fresh air surrounding the clear water was like a tranquilizer, the wild roses were in bloom, and the company was—well, he hadn't had to worry about the baby after all. The little girl had fallen asleep on the drive to the lake and now she lay dreaming peacefully on a blanket, her arms and legs tucked beneath her, her tiny baby behind hitched into the air. When she was awake, she was a danger, needing constant protection and care and nurturing, all things he knew little of. But asleep, she was safe to watch, and he found her intriguing. Like a puppy at the pound that he could look at and admire but would never think of bringing home.

The fact that he was even thinking of this child with fascination bothered him since he knew it *was* merely simple fascination, the very thing that had induced his parents to have children and then neglect them. Still, he knew he would never do the same thing, and so, for the moment, he simply enjoyed.

Caroline—who'd given him this day—was sitting there, smiling that dreamy, blue-eyed smile that made his heart twist and his body throb with need.

"Look at the sun going down. Have you ever seen anything so ripe and perfect?"

He had. He was looking at her right now. And when she turned to see if he had heard her, he knew that she had read his mind—or, at least, his expression.

"You're so very lovely," he told her. "I think perhaps it was a mistake to hire you. Not for me, mind you. You're doing all the things I wanted you to do, and doing them well, but I seem to have this urge to touch you. That can't be a good thing."

"Because there's no future in it," she agreed.

"Yes, that. And also—"

"Because you don't really want to be attracted to me. It bothers you that you are."

She said the words simply, without emotion, but he could feel the wound beneath. She'd had far too many

Bobby Cummingses in her life, he suspected. Men who were enchanted by her charm and her looks and the very life that almost burst from her every minute of the day. Men who had hurt her somehow. If he knew how, there were probably plenty of men in town whom he'd want to take apart. He didn't want to be another man hurting her. But he could see that the very fact that he kept moving toward her and backing away was taking its toll.

So he opened his mouth to share his secret. Maybe it was a secret she wouldn't want to know, one he shouldn't reveal. He'd never talked about this with anyone. Ever. Even Erin hadn't really wanted to discuss it. It was too painful.

But he had hurt Caroline somehow because of incidents in his past that he had to live with, and so she should know.

"My father was a greedy man," he said slowly, gently.

"He was rich," she said, telling him all that she apparently knew of the man. "You said he was in real estate."

"Yes, and he was greedy there. He wanted to own everything, I think. But in this case, I'm not talking about property or money. My father wanted women. Many women. He had a tendency to hire young, beautiful maids, nannies, housekeepers, cooks—women he found physically attractive."

"Is that why you hired Paula?"

He froze for a second, but he looked directly into her eyes. "I wasn't attracted to Paula. In fact, I've made a habit of hiring women who don't attract me. Paula was—I didn't know I was hurting her until I'd already done it. She felt something I didn't return. I let her go because it wouldn't have been right to keep her once I realized the truth.''

''You found her other work.''

''Yes.''

''And she cried about you to the whole town. That wasn't very nice of her.''

He dismissed her words with a quick wave of his hand. ''My fault. I've lived with the master-servant relationship long enough to recognize the dangers. I should have seen it coming and ended things sooner, and—''

She waited.

He raised his head, looked right into her eyes until he thought he would stop breathing forever. ''—I'm attracted to you. Tremendously. I shouldn't have hired you.''

''But you did.''

''Yes. I was short on time, and…I let my need for the most qualified and competent helper block out the fact that I knew it would be a mistake to bring you this close.''

''Why are you telling me this now, Gideon?''

He turned his head to the side. ''Because you gave me this day. Because I should have been honest with you from the start. And also because you deserve better than what you're getting.''

''And what am I getting?''

He had to be honest with her. ''A man who's complicating your summer by his desire to touch you.''

''And what am I giving you?''

He took a deep strengthening breath. ''An excellent job done with a smile and a great deal of grace and good humor.''

''And frustration,'' she told him simply.

He jerked his head around. "And frustration," he agreed. "But that's my problem."

"And if I'm frustrated, too?"

The silence was long and dangerous and chilling.

"We both know nothing good could come out of getting involved," Gideon continued. "My relationships are always…simple and I feel a need to keep them that way. Yours, I suspect, are more complex. It would be the height of stupidity for us to act on our frustration."

Her smile trembled, but it held. "I'm glad to hear you say that again, because we both know we don't suit. But we're here, Gideon. Together. And we're in this frustration thing together, too. So let's just admit it exists. Besides, we only slipped once. We both survived that kiss. We're doing fine."

He wanted to howl at that thought. Right now it was only gravity and sheer will power that was keeping him from joining her on the other side of the tablecloth and sampling those sweet berry lips of hers again. But she was smiling so bravely. As if she didn't even know that he wanted her at all.

He body-blocked his desire. "You had other things you wanted to discuss," he said, reaching for safe ground.

Caroline blinked at the change in subject. "Yes, your sister will be here in a week, Gideon. And I'm a bit…nervous. I think I might have mentioned that."

"Once or twice." He smiled.

"So I need suggestions. How does one entertain the privileged? The theatre? museums? shopping? a party?"

"Why are you nervous, Caroline?" he asked gently. "Those ideas are perfect."

She took a deep breath. "A party then. At the end of

her visit. In two weeks. Something small since there isn't much time. A few of your business associates?''

He nodded his agreement, smiling more broadly as she began to count on her fingers. ''Maybe a few of your friends as well.''

''Thank you. I'd feel more comfortable.'' And she knew that was just what he'd intended. ''Unfortunately, I doubt Rebecca and Emily will be available. Emily is planning a party of her own for her employer's aunt's birthday bash and Rebecca will be deep in the throes of helping Logan handle his hotel's grand opening right around then. I'll think of a few others.''

''Invite some men, won't you?'' he asked, picking up a brownie and devouring it in a few quick bites. ''Did you bake these?''

She nodded. ''Mrs. Williams let me in the kitchen for awhile. You want another?''

He smiled a dazzling smile. ''Don't twist my arm, sweetheart. This is heaven you can hold in your hand. You could take over the world with these brownies,'' he confided.

''How do you know I'm not?'' she asked. ''Starting with you. Before the day is out, I could have you signing over all your worldly goods to me.''

''Hmm. Might be worth it,'' he admitted, taking another bite. ''So I'll invite some colleagues. You'll invite some people you know, too.''

''I will. You said men?''

''And women.''

''Yes. But the men—you want some of my male friends to entertain the women your sister is bringing to meet you.''

He tried to look innocent.

She laughed out loud. "All right. I'll invite men. I know one or two."

Was that a frown that crossed his lips just before he popped the rest of the brownie into his mouth? She wasn't sure. Probably not.

"You should let your sister know we're having a small dinner party, though," she told him. "No one likes to walk into a surprise situation blind."

He looked up at her from beneath those long lashes, his gray eyes suddenly laser sharp and intense.

"I didn't mean me—or our situation," she said quickly. "I knew that someone would buy me that day."

"Yes, but you got a bit more than you bargained for, didn't you, Caroline? I'll bet there was no other employer who would have asked so much or caused you so many problems."

He was right. Absolutely right. Any other employer would have been simpler, safer. Any other man wouldn't have made her want to lick the brownie crumbs from his lips.

She sucked in a deep breath and began packing up their picnic items, trying to manage her thoughts. "No one else would have been so generous, either, Gideon. We're managing," she said, brushing at the wrinkles in her shorts as she rose to her feet.

She looked at him and saw that his gaze had focused on the movement of her hands over her body. He shook his head as if to clear his thoughts, rose to his feet and picked up the basket.

"We'll manage," he said a bit too firmly. "I'll call my sister and clear the party with her. And I'll—thank you for the picnic, Caroline. I think I needed it."

She smiled. The thought that she could give a man as

rich as Gideon something he needed with something as simple as a picnic seemed ludicrous, but maybe she was wrong. She had the feeling he hadn't shared many picnics as a child, and he was looking more relaxed than he had in days.

Well, she *was* here to help. To help his sister realize he was content. So maybe she needed to work on Gideon's contentment level, on helping him relax. The fact that his smile was part of the equation was just a nice bonus. As long as she was careful not to get too close or to fall under his spell.

The baby had awakened by the time they had returned to Tremayne Hall, and Gideon could no longer ignore her soft little yawns. Caroline leaned into the back seat of the car.

"We're home, love," she whispered, smiling at the baby waving the plastic keys she'd been rattling. The little girl held up her hands and puckered her lips, and the keys fell to the ground.

"Yes, kissing is what we do when we love," Caroline admitted, and Gideon noted with interest the pink sheen along her jaw. "And sometimes when we just like. Umm, I think there's a clean spot right…here," Caroline said, lifting the child and ducking her head to kiss the child's cheek as well as her lips. For two seconds she was hidden from his view, long enough to banish the blush, he noted. "Looks like we need some water for your toy, Lib."

The little girl gurgled, but instead of turning toward the house, Caroline headed for the fountain at the far side of the sloping lawn.

The baby's eyes lit up. She chortled and bucked.

Caroline laughed and turned toward Gideon.

"Ever dance in a fountain? Or at least dangle your feet in one?" she asked, and that I've-got-a-secret mischievous look on her face won him over completely.

"Come to think of it, I haven't."

"You have a fountain like this and you haven't even tried it?"

His smile deepened. "I do feel ashamed to admit it. My favorite fountain, too."

"And very lovely," she agreed. "Quite beautiful in fact with all these lush green lawns stretching around it. You know, you really should make use of your grounds. You've been working too hard. Mrs. Williams agrees. It's why she made us the picnic."

Gideon rubbed the hard line of his jaw. Of course he didn't believe for a moment that Mrs. Williams had any interest in how much he worked, but this lady obviously cared. The way she cared about anyone and everyone, and so he would do this childish thing she was asking of him. Gideon reached down and began to peel off his shoes and socks. He rolled up the legs of his pants and sat on the edge of the fountain. Caroline had already settled herself there, her long, bare legs golden beneath her coral shorts, the baby carefully tucked beside her.

Gideon sank his feet into the cool shallow water while the warm sun shone down on his head, and felt the tension slipping away like ice cubes melting in the sun. He closed his eyes, tipped his head back.

He heard her low chuckle. "People probably pay good money at a spa for just this kind of pleasure," she said.

Then she fell silent. So did he. For long minutes the only sound was of the occasional bird and the baby's soft liquid babble. Heaven should be like this, he thought for one crazy second before he chased the thought away and opened his eyes to turn toward the woman across from him. She was looking at him, her eyelids fluttering as if he'd startled her or caught her doing something wrong and sinful. As if she were embarrassed to be discovered studying him. She quickly turned toward the child.

"Okay, enough sun for you, honeybunch," the lady said. "Your sunblock will be wearing off, and we don't want any baby French fries. Come on, once around the fountain and you and I are done."

He heard the soft splash, but even if he hadn't, he would have felt that she had gone from the place where she'd been, sitting three feet to his right. He was that aware of her, day and night. And it was the most natural thing in the world to rise to his feet and amble toward her. She and Libby were catching the flow of the fountain in their hands, flinging the water out in bright, sparkling drops, although the baby kept trying to sit down in the water.

"No. No, angel," Caroline said sweetly. "Not today." Then they went back to their walking and splashing. He joined them, enjoying the sight of them making use of his fountain until a big splash of water hit him full in the face.

Startled, he sputtered, slung his head, and looked down into the suddenly shocked and frightened eyes of the child.

His breath froze in his lungs, he schooled his face to remain expressionless, but Caroline was already hustling the baby off to the side of the fountain.

"We have to be careful. No water in the face, Libby. Okay?"

The little girl just stared, and Caroline tenderly lifted her out and over the side.

"It's okay, Caroline. It's just water."

Caroline looked up at Gideon. The careful gentleness in his tone made her heart turn to soft cream. She knew he didn't feel comfortable with Libby, but he was going to work very hard not to let it show too much. For that she was grateful. Too grateful, evidently, for in that moment she forgot Libby's tendency to hug and kiss. While she was still leaning forward over the side, the little girl reached up for her, throwing her off balance.

Afraid she would fall forward onto the baby, she leaned back. But she leaned too far, ending up sitting on her bottom in six inches of water, with droplets of water in her hair, and on her face.

The little girl giggled from her place on relatively safe ground. "No," Libby drawled.

Caroline looked up to see the big man beside her trying to stifle a smile. He looked down at her and she followed his gaze. Her shorts were still dry and pale in only a few places. Great splash stains had formed on major portions of her cream-colored blouse.

"It's only water, love," he told her solemnly, but looking like he wanted to grin. "But you might want to get changed just the same. Sitting might be most uncomfortable for a while after this."

She chuckled, shaking her head and holding up one hand for him to help her up. Then she was against him, and he was warm where she was wet, hot where she was dry.

They both stepped back at the same moment. She climbed from the fountain, reached for Libby, then realized she couldn't lift the little girl without soaking her totally.

"Go get changed. You're going to start shivering now that the sun's going down. We'll make our way back."

Caroline raised a brow. She started to open her mouth.

"It's only a few steps. You'll hurry and be taking over soon," he assured her.

She would. He had offered—very nicely—but she knew that he avoided babies the way other people avoided tall trees in thunderstorms.

She had made a promise when she'd brought Libby here that she'd never give him reason to regret it. And she wouldn't.

The one hundred feet from the fountain to the house was going to seem like a thousand, Gideon thought, taking the tiny little hand in his own. Should he walk with her? Should he dare try to pick her up?

The very idea was simply unthinkable. He looked down at her. She looked back up at him. Solemnly, and yet not fearfully.

They walked.

He could feel the small fingers nestling in his palm. Trusting. The very thought was enough to make a grown man quake.

He looked down at her again.

And found her staring back.

"Libby. It's a pretty name" was all he said. As if to himself. As if he and this child weren't in any way connected.

She smiled, with those big blue eyes, with all of her. He'd seen her smile before, at Caroline, at Roy, even at Mrs. Williams. But not at him.

She was smiling at him.

He wanted to run, to still the furious pounding of his heart. He wanted to let go of her hand, but she was a baby, and he couldn't do that.

They kept walking. Slowly. So slowly. Because she was relatively new to this walking business. He didn't want to make her trip.

That was why, he supposed, Caroline was already coming toward them by the time they made it to the house.

Relief flooded his soul. And something else as well. A small reluctance to have this moment end.

He looked down at the child. "We made it," he said, and chuckled.

Libby grinned up at him.

It was what he'd wanted, he realized. To see if he could make her smile again.

For a moment he reveled in that smile.

And then the enormity of what he was doing hit him. He was treating her like a toy. And he knew he had to be careful here. It was so easy to be caught up in the "baby package," the infectious laughter, the melting smiles, the petal-soft skin and baby-powder scent. But another very important part of that package was a little ego as fragile as a melting snowflake. She was so vulnerable. The mere thought that someone could wipe that trusting little smile away was chilling. And it could be done. Without a thought, maybe even without the knowledge that harm was being done. Simply by turning away, or not being what she needed the adults in her life to be. He knew about adults who couldn't really be parents. He knew that coldness. It had grown in him. It was a part of him, just like his hands. And he was incapable of true, deep and lasting warmth, the absolute commitment that a child just had to have.

So thank goodness he would never know that kind of haunting responsibility that a baby like this would require. He would never have to worry about hurting a child.

This child was special. All children were special, but he would never have a child.

What's more, very soon this little girl and Caroline would simply be a part of his past. Surely, that was a good thing. If it didn't feel that way right now, it would in time. That was just the way things had to be. For their sakes…and his.

Chapter Seven

"Erin, I just called to tell you to bring your dancing shoes," Gideon declared later that night. "We're planning a dinner party in your honor."

"We?" The speculative hum in his sister's voice stood out like a lighthouse in the fog. Trust Erin to ignore the main news and zero in on the details.

"I—I have a new assistant," he said noncommittally. "She thought I might consider your own wishes before I started making plans." He chuckled.

"You must have told her how bossy I am, little brother," she said with a laugh.

"Absolutely, sweet stuff."

The silence on the other end of the line was like a living thing.

"Is that the sound of you sticking your tongue out at me—I hope?" he demanded.

"No, you dolt. It's the sound of me wiping tears from my eyes. I miss you, Gid. It's been too long since we've seen each other. And look, without me there to help you out, you're having to hire assistants. Prim sorts who think you have to check with me just to decide whether or not to throw a party. Is she pretty? Wait, don't answer that. I know you never hire anyone pretty. The only beautiful people in your life are the women you sleep with. What's wrong with us, Gideon? Why can't you and I have normal, healthy love lives like everyone else?''

''You will. I feel it,'' he said. And he hoped it was so.

''And you?''

''Umm, that's not me. You know that.''

He could hear her blowing out her breath in frustration. ''When you meet the right woman, Gideon…''

''I'll hire her,'' he promised. ''To cook and clean for me. But for now, Mrs. Williams will have to do.''

Silence again. ''You never change, Gideon. Will you ever?''

''I promise I won't, love.''

''At least we'll always have each other, Gid.''

''That we will, brat.''

More silence.

''That was me smiling this time, Gideon. I can't wait to see you face-to-face again. And all right, tell your assistant that I'd love a party.''

But as he hung up the phone, he heard a soft tapping on the door and his ''assistant'' was there with her arms full.

He took the pitcher of daisies from Caroline and found her lovely face hiding behind them.

''Flowers?'' he asked.

''Yes. I just thought—well, you spend so much time

in here working—I just thought—you might like some color?'' she offered. ''A reminder that there's a very pretty world outside your windows?''

''Taking care of me, Caroline?''

''Your sister has a point about your not taking care of yourself, you know. If you really want to convince her that you're fine, you'll need to show her that you're seeing to your own needs. And I don't mean consuming barely edible food and water to stay alive,'' she argued, when he started to protest.

''So I need daisies?''

She nodded. ''You need color and life. Brownies from time to time, a dance in a fountain.''

He looked at the other object she was holding. ''And that? What is it?''

''A picture of clouds, of course.'' And she held out the wild, art-deco print she was carrying. It was all bright reds and blues and yellows.

''Like real clouds, if you look at it long enough, you can see things in it. The face of a woman. Maybe a tree. Depends on your mood.''

''And I need this?'' He could barely contain his grin.

''You need it. Gideon, I'm sure your clients are wonderful people, but…there's more to life than work.''

''I'll try to remember that. And Caroline? Thank you.''

She gazed up into his eyes in that way that made him ache to move closer. Every time. That look she was giving him kept him awake half the night, every night.

''You're a good man, Gideon,'' she whispered. And her words pushed him over the edge. He drew her near, slipped his fingers beneath her hair and allowed himself just the briefest taste of her lips. Soft. Sweet. Achingly tender and sensitive. He brushed her lips with his own, then let her go.

"Erin says—" His voice was thick, colored with the feelings touching her had stirred in him. "—Erin says she'd love a dinner party."

She nodded silently, cradling the hand he'd held to pull her close. Then she turned to go.

Clutching the doorknob, she looked back over her shoulder.

"Maybe—maybe we should ask your sister if she'd like to be involved in the planning. It would take her mind off her own problems. People get caught up in these things, they become a part of the process. It can be very therapeutic."

He managed a brief nod. He thought he said that he'd ask Erin, but he wasn't sure he'd actually voiced the words. All he knew was that as Caroline left the room, she had touched her fingers to her lips in a brief unconscious gesture. As if he'd wounded her, hurt her where his mouth had grazed hers.

He cursed himself for losing control with her again, and he wondered if hiring Caroline was the most wonderful or the most foolish thing he'd ever done. Either way, he was going to have to wrap a noose around those errant urges he felt whenever she entered his territory. He was starting to act just way too much like a male going down for the last time. It felt both agonizingly frightening and absolutely exhilarating.

And his sister was coming. A woman who missed nothing.

The woman was driving him crazy, and she hadn't even done anything. He hadn't either, Gideon admitted.

It had been four days since he'd last kissed her.

But kissing Caroline lingered with a man, and the beast had been unleashed. Now, everywhere he turned, she was in his mind. Caroline feeding him brownies she'd made herself. The lady wet and blue-eyed innocent and part of his thoughts all the time.

All he had to see was Roy trailing after her to make him want to suggest the young man keep another ten feet between him and Caroline. And when he heard her laughter, he had the strongest urge to go see what had amused her.

He wondered if this was the way it had started with his father and the women he employed, this fierce hunger that made it difficult to think—and work.

"And if he did, that's just too damn bad, Tremayne," he warned himself. Caroline had a solid plan for her life. It involved children and loving and giving, even if, as she claimed, she wasn't looking for romance. He also had a plan for his life, and marriage and family weren't on the itinerary.

So he stayed away as much as he could. Only now, well, damn it, much as he didn't want to notice, he couldn't help seeing just how nervous she was about his sister's arrival a week from now. She was working at sixty miles an hour twenty-four hours a day, seven days a week. And that was on top of taking care of that little, round, blue-eyed pixie of a niece of hers. Not that he knew *anything* but...darn it, she *was* a baby, and babies required specialized attention. A woman couldn't see to a child's needs *and* work herself to death at the same time.

"So? You're the boss, aren't you?" he asked himself. "Step in. Do something to ease her mind."

He tried. When he found her that afternoon, he told her that Erin had been ecstatic about the idea of the party when he'd called.

"We'll see" was all she'd say. "I'm working on the plans. I'm having the gold satin drapes that partitioned off a part of the ballroom cleaned. Since this will be a small group, I thought we might use them. Make the room all gold and blue and white. With lots of candles. Very romantic."

She peered up at him from beneath long lashes, biting her lower lip just a bit.

He nearly groaned aloud.

"Just in case your sister is a romantic sort. I'm not, of course, but she or her friends might be."

Gideon raised one brow. "I'm sure she'll love it."

She took a long, deep, visible breath. "I found boxes and boxes of antique ball gowns and uniforms and men's jackets. Do you think—I'm talking strictly as a drama teacher here—I do have an interest in costume, but these were your mother's things. Do you think your sister would be interested in them? They're beautiful museum pieces, actually, but they've been packed away for so long…"

What he really thought was that Erin would have absolutely no interest in anything his mother might have kept. But Caroline's eyes were glowing. Sparkling. Heartbreakingly lovely. He could tell that her romantic soul was conjuring up visions of lords and ladies of years past, twirling around a ballroom. This was the heart of who she was, and he couldn't risk dismissing or destroying that, even if he had no clue what he would do with a mountain of antique clothing.

"Why don't we see if there's someone in town who can restore them? I'm sure Erin will be entranced." He'd make sure his sister said nothing that would spoil the dream.floating through Caroline's mind.

"Thank you, you're a kind man, Gideon," she said, deep gratitude in her eyes, and he knew that she was aware that his actions weren't all for his sister.

The blue of her eyes was so intense that for a second he had to curl his fingers into fists, and keep his feet from carrying him forward to take her into his arms. He looked away to compose himself and noticed that they weren't quite alone.

Libby cooed at him from the safe area of blankets and toys Caroline had set up a few feet away. The baby smiled up at him. She giggled, and then went back to her toys. He realized that he'd been holding his breath.

Caroline caught the catch in his breath when Gideon looked at Libby. A pain shivered through her heart, and she cursed his parents who hadn't given him love. He'd surgically removed that emotion from his life, but he still knew he had the power to damage another child—and he would never do that. If the only way to keep from harming someone was to remain aloof, that's what he'd do. She'd do well to remember that. This was not a man she could have a cozy friendship with, or make babies with.

Right now the man was looking around at the warm wood and green and gold accents of the morning room. Anything but the baby or her, Caroline noted.

He ran his fingers over the gleaming carved wood trim framing the door. "You've worked a bit of a miracle here," he said. "I'm impressed."

She hazarded a smile to let him know she and Libby were okay. "It's a lovely room. Just needed a bit of attention."

"Which you've been giving it. Practically nonstop."

"There's a lot to be done and time is running pitifully short. So I've been cleaning, decorating, reading—books on etiquette, mostly. The lives of the rich and famous. How to throw killer dinner parties. I'll be ready soon." She hoped he hadn't heard the doubt in her voice. She'd played many roles before, but this one was too real. It would last a whole twenty-four hours a day. She was pretty sure that Erin Tremayne knew the ins and outs of etiquette without even having to cram.

Still, Caroline knew Gideon had hired her because he had faith in her ability. She would just have to deliver.

He studied her carefully. "You're doing a wonderful job here, Caroline, just as I thought you would. That doesn't mean I want you to give up eating and sleeping."

She rolled her eyes. "You see me at dinner every night." And they had very careful conversations, staying well away from the topic of babies, marriage or touching.

"You're eating," he conceded. "But you're still working too hard without a break. If you need more assistants…"

She held up one hand. "Roy is all I need."

Gideon quirked up one brow.

Caroline smiled in spite of herself. "Okay, I do have to stay on my toes around Roy, even if he's a dream of a helper. But not enough assistants isn't the problem, Gideon. I just like doing…everything."

"Then do a little more. Take the afternoon off. Go have some fun. Get out of the house."

"I don't think—"

"Your niece—" he began.

Caroline waited.

"—the baby would probably like an outing."

And you'd like me—and her—out of your way for awhile. The thought saddened her, even knowing what she knew about him. Caroline squared her shoulders. She raised her chin a bit.

"You're the boss," she said quietly, trying to keep all emotion from her voice. "Libby and I will take a field trip."

A trace of a smile appeared on Gideon's lips.

"Why do I have the feeling that I know exactly how Bobby Cummings felt when you kicked him in the shins?" he asked.

"He deserved it," she said.

"He deserved it," Gideon agreed. "And so do I if I've hurt your feelings."

She melted. "I know. I understand. I really do."

"I just don't want you to work yourself into the ground."

"I won't. Really," she said when he gave her one of those long, lazy, incredulous smiles.

"And you'll take some time for you and your... charge when you both need it."

"I said we would go."

"Good then. Take my car. Yours was listing the last time you drove it," he said, holding out the keys.

She hesitated. "Gideon..."

"I trust you with my car," he said. "And it's more reliable and safer than yours."

"You haven't had cookie crumbs in your Porsche yet. It's not really a 'baby' car."

He sucked in a breath, raised himself to his full six-two and turned his hand palm up, still offering the keys.

''We'll try not to do too much damage to it,'' she promised with an apologetic smile.

Libby gurgled as if in agreement. She had wandered over to Caroline and was peeking out from behind her aunt's legs, only the top of her head and her eyes showing. Gideon's eyes slid down to look at her, then moved quickly back up to Caroline's face. As if even acknowledging the baby's presence would be a mistake.

''She doesn't bite,'' Caroline said softly.

''I'm sure she doesn't,'' Gideon agreed, but he didn't let his gaze wander toward the baby again.

''And neither do I, Gideon. You and I are doing fine. I've almost forgotten that we ever kissed. We're out of the danger zone, I think.''

His eyes turned fierce and hot.

''I'm barely keeping the lid on my control, Caroline. Don't—just don't let down your guard.''

With that warning, he wished her and Libby a good outing and left.

''The man knows how to make an exit, Libby,'' she whispered. But her flippant response wouldn't fly. He was right to warn her. When she left Tremayne Hall, she didn't want to be looking over her shoulder. She didn't want to make any unforgettable memories with the man. And she'd already made more than one, because she'd lied. The memory of Gideon's lips roaming her body still woke her in hot, aching dreams.

So the woman had almost forgotten they'd kissed. Well, that was good. Absolutely, Gideon reminded himself, glancing out the window for the ninth time in as many minutes. He wanted to forget her, too, but there she was, dead in his sights on the long sloping lawn of his property.

She certainly hadn't been gone long. Just long enough to secure a kite and some string, apparently. For the last ten minutes, she and the baby had been running full tilt trying to get the kite to stay aloft, seemingly unconcerned that the less-than-windy day wasn't really cooperating. The fun seemed to be merely in the act of trying.

As he watched the baby clap her hands while Caroline did her best to play the kite, Gideon couldn't help but smile. He had a tremendous urge to go down there and join them. Not that he'd spent much time with such things as a child. His mother would have considered a kite the toy of the lower classes, and his father wouldn't have had the time or inclination to show him how to fly one. Neither of them would have cared how he felt.

And how did he feel right now watching Caroline?

"Don't travel that path, Tremayne," he warned himself, forcing his eyes back to the computer screen. "You've already had a discussion with the lady and she very sensibly suggested putting all that behind us."

Which he would gladly do, if he could just start forgetting the feel of her bare skin beneath his fingers. If he could just stop remembering the flavor of her lips and how she'd sighed against him when his tongue had stroked hers.

A long row of T's appeared on his screen when he held the key down too long.

"Get your mind back on business," he ordered himself.

And for a full fifteen minutes, he almost managed to do just that.

Until he looked up and saw Caroline had finished her game with the child and gone inside. Until he realized she had returned alone and was climbing an old oak tree to retrieve the kite tangled in the branches of a trembling limb.

His fingers went flat on the keys. His heart did a drop-dead stop. The door slammed against the wall as he pushed it aside and shot down the hall and out onto the lawn.

He wanted to call her name, to warn her to stay still until he could reach her, but he tossed that idea aside. If he startled her, she might slip.

Then she looked down.

''Gideon, you're here,'' she said, smiling softly at him. ''You missed all the fun.''

From her perch ten feet above his head, he had a delicious view of long, shapely, bare legs. Her smile was an angel's and he could gladly have wrung her neck.

''Caroline, that branch isn't all that stable. Don't move.''

She wrinkled her nose. ''I'm not that high, Gideon, and I've been climbing trees forever. This branch will hold me.''

''Until you slip.''

''I won't. Just let me get Libby's kite.'' She turned away as if he weren't even there. His heart labored every time he saw the branch sway a millimeter. Wrapping one arm around the main trunk, she inched out along the limb, lifted her other arm over her head and freed the kite. It drifted down to the ground like a top-heavy bird.

"All right, I'm coming down," she said, looking down into his eyes and smiling gently. "I'll be right there."

He watched her descend, every move, every careful step. Until her foot slipped slightly and she was forced to catch at the trunk and steady herself.

He didn't stop to think. He was up the lower branches of the tree in a tenth of a heartbeat. She'd caught herself already, but he still placed one hand around her waist.

"I'm sure you're an expert at this, Caroline," he whispered, "but have some pity—I haven't spent years watching you. Take it slowly coming down. I'll be right below to break your fall if I should need to."

"You won't," she promised.

"Humor me, Caroline," he urged.

She nodded. "I'll be careful. Really."

Then he was on the ground, reaching up for her.

She let herself slide down the last few feet into his arms. He found her waist with his hands and pulled her to safety on the ground below. Only when she was folded into his arms did he take a deep breath.

"Caroline, you must have driven your parents mad," he whispered near her ear.

"Sometimes," she whispered back.

"You're driving *me* mad," he confessed.

"Because you want to kiss me and yet you don't want to."

"I know it's a mistake," he agreed.

Yet his fear and his want had the best of him right now. He dragged her against him, felt the warm, pulsing life flow through her, bent her back and took her lips.

She wrapped her arms tightly around him, kissing him

back, moving her lips to his jaw, his neck, burrowing against him and making the connection even closer.

''We said we wouldn't do this,'' she said, as his mouth hovered over her own again.

''We won't. Not after this,'' he promised.

''No, we won't. This is just a reaction—because you thought I might fall—because my heart skidded a little bit when I slipped,'' she agreed, tilting her head back so his mouth could drift down over her chin, her throat, into the vee of her blouse.

''It's a reaction,'' he agreed, his chest expanding as he breathed in deeply, loosened his hold on her and brushed his lips over hers one more time.

She could feel him hovering on the brink. Of taking this deeper, moving it farther along.

But he didn't really want to, she knew. He would regret it. And so would she.

So she dredged up her deepest grin. She disengaged herself from his arms, and pretended to study her extremities.

''All in one piece,'' she said triumphantly. ''But thank you for the assist, Gideon. Guess I'm a bit out of shape.''

He arched one wicked, mocking brow and she wrinkled her nose.

''I was talking about my ability to climb trees.''

He took the cue, grinned back gamely. ''You probably would have made it down all right. You seemed like a pro to me, Caroline. I just haven't spent a lot of time watching people climb trees.''

The statement caught Caroline off guard. Every kid she knew growing up had practically lived in trees in the summer—until they'd gotten old enough to notice the opposite sex. Then they'd spent most of their time trying to get each other's attention.

She wondered just exactly what Gideon's childhood had been like. And she would continue to wonder, but at another time, she realized, because at the moment there was someone walking toward them.

Not a toddler. Not a young man. Not an elderly servant. A woman. Lovely and dark-haired and slender and smiling. And flanked by two other women.

Caroline tensed.

"Gideon," the woman called, speeding up her pace.

Caroline looked at Gideon. He looked both delighted and perturbed.

"Erin," he said slowly, softly.

Caroline didn't know whether to look down at her disheveled clothing and her bare feet or at the house, where things were still in a state of semi-disarray.

But she felt Gideon's hand on her wrist as he gently tugged her forward, taking the decision out of her hands. She raised her other hand and pushed her tumble of hair back out of her eyes, trying to smooth it. She managed to step away a pace or two so that it didn't look like she was practically in Gideon's embrace. She hoped.

Then the petite, dark-haired beauty in pale yellow was launching herself at Gideon.

"Oh Gid, it's good to see you. No, it's great to see you. I've missed you so much," his sister said with a cry. She hugged him hard as her feet came off the ground.

"Erin," he drawled with obvious affection, gently wiping her tears away with his handkerchief. "I'm glad you're here. I've missed you, too, brat."

"Brat," she said, wrinkling her nose. "And I'm his

older sister, too,'' she told the two women who had come up behind her. She let her glance trail from her friends, a gorgeous honey-blonde and a willowy ebony-haired beauty, to Caroline. Her eyes opened just a touch wider, and Caroline nervously glanced to Gideon who was grinning.

Caroline wished she had her shoes on. She would kill right this moment for a comb to push through her hair. She hoped and prayed that her lipstick wasn't smeared and her dress wasn't too wrinkled.

''Erin, allow me to present Caroline O'Donald. She's pitching in while we have guests.''

Caroline forced her terror aside and called forth her stage presence. She smiled at Gideon's sister who was regarding her a bit uncertainly. Holding out one hand to Erin, she was relieved to find that the woman's hand-shake was not limp and condescending.

''Please excuse my appearance,'' Caroline said in the same voice she'd used for the socialite she'd portrayed in the last school play. ''But my niece lost her kite in the tree. Gideon very generously helped me retrieve it and it was a bit of an awkward task.''

''You're Gideon's assistant?'' There was a definite trace of disbelief in the woman's voice, but she quickly masked it and managed a gracious smile.

''Yes. Yes, I am,'' Caroline concurred, standing tall and as proud as she could, given her situation. ''And I've been looking forward to meeting you, Ms. Tre-mayne, especially since my chief purpose here is to make sure your visit is a pleasant one. I hope you'll feel free to let me know if there's anything you or your guests need.''

Erin raised one brow in that same way her brother

had. "I'm so glad to meet you, Ms. O'Donald, and very pleased that Gideon has finally hired someone to help him take care of things at the family fortress. But please, I hope you'll feel free to call me Erin and forgive me for descending on you a full week ahead of when you expected me. When Gideon called last night, I realized that I just couldn't wait to see him. Please, let me introduce you to my friends, Danielle Alberts and Sonia Duvree."

By then, Roy had come sauntering up with Libby, fresh from her nap. The baby began to engage in a game of peekaboo with the honey-blonde, Danielle.

"Ah, you've made a friend for life," Caroline warned, smiling at the woman and shaking both her hand and the somewhat shy Sonia's as well.

"She's a dear," Danielle cooed, just as Libby came out from hiding and began tugging on the lady's frothy, shimmery skirt. Clearly the baby wasn't done with the game yet.

Caroline heard Gideon's low chuckle just before she noticed the woman's skirt slipping slightly, and she hurriedly bent down and scooped Libby up.

"I'm sorry, Ms. Alberts. No, love," she said firmly.

"No," Libby agreed, and she puckered up her lips.

Caroline kissed her, holding her protectively close lest anyone should have been offended. For a second, she thought she felt Gideon almost mirror her move as he stepped slightly closer to her. But that was a silly thought, of course, when Libby made him cold-palmed nervous, and he knew very well that she herself was more than capable of handling things.

And she was, Caroline reminded herself, turning back to the newcomers. She noticed the way Sonia was gazing worshipfully up at Gideon. She also noticed the way Erin was looking from her to the baby to Gideon.

"I'm sorry. My sister has enlisted my help with her daughter while she's out of town on business," Caroline quickly explained. She wanted very badly to explain that she and Gideon had just met and that she was "just an assistant." Instead, she practiced her gracious smile.

"She's a beautiful baby," Erin declared warmly.

"Yes, I think so," Caroline said softly. "But you don't need me to keep you standing around talking about babies right now. Why don't we go back to the house so I can show you to your rooms and see about having some food sent up? Once you're settled and fed, I can fill you in on what kind of recreation is available in the area, and you can let me know how I can make this trip more enjoyable for you."

"It's an awfully gorgeous mansion," Sonia was cooing to Gideon. "You must love it. You must have a lot of room here."

"A great deal," he agreed, smiling gently at the obviously besotted woman. "And Caroline knows all about the house. More than I do, actually, since she has a bit of a…history with it."

"You'll tell us some stories then, won't you?" Erin asked, smiling at Caroline. "My father bought this house, but I'm not very familiar with it."

"Most of what I know is purely speculation," Caroline began hesitantly. "The house was uninhabited for long periods of time even before your family purchased it."

"Speculation? Sounds like fun. You'll share?" Erin said with a chuckle.

Caroline nodded. "What I know, I'll share."

"Then for now I'll leave all of you in Caroline's capable hands," Gideon announced. "Welcome home again, brat. It's been way too long," he said, giving his sister one last hug. "See you soon."

At his last words, he looked over his sister's head to Caroline to include her.

Honestly, how on earth was she going to be able to keep reminding herself that she was just an employee if the man kept on looking at her like that and being so darn nice? No wonder Sonia's eyes were practically rolling around in her head. The man was just lethally charming. For her own part, she needed to remember that the past two weeks were over, and her last week, her performance week, had begun.

"I'll take good care of them, Gideon," she said, sticking to her role.

"I never doubted it," he told her as they all moved away. "I'll stop and see Mrs. Williams about finding something for Libby's afternoon snack. It's time, isn't it?"

Caroline realized in that moment that Libby was sucking on her fist, a sure sign that she was hungry. How strange that Gideon who felt so uncomfortable around children should have noticed the little girl's need when she had not.

Chapter Eight

Gideon was walking down the hallway with Erin the next morning when his sister skidded to a stop.

"We didn't look in here yesterday when Caroline took us on a tour," she explained pushing a door open before Gideon could stop her.

"Let's come back another time, Erin," he coaxed. He knew why Caroline had excluded this room. It was the one she hadn't had a chance to finish. His sister's early arrival had caught her off guard. Him, too, he thought, remembering how he'd just finished kissing her silly right before his sister had shown up.

"It's the ballroom," Erin whispered, in awe as she entered the room. "Of course you knew that. Oh, Gideon, it's gorgeous, isn't it? And there's your Caroline."

In a heartbeat Gideon was through the doorway.

Caroline was on her knees before a box at the other end of the room. As they crossed the floor, she quickly rose.

"I—I thought I'd better finish up," she said, holding out her hands to indicate the room. "There's still a bit left to do." Her tone was apologetic, and no way was Gideon going to have her taking the blame for something that wasn't her fault.

"But you've already done so much in the time you've had," he pointed out. "And it's spectacular. Don't you agree, Erin? Caroline has spent the last eleven days putting as much of the house in order as she can. This room was quite a challenge. A bit of a mess, actually, until she worked her magic on it."

Erin was gazing up at him speculatively. He ignored "the look." Caroline deserved every one of those compliments.

"It's absolutely exquisite," his sister agreed. "I was in here just briefly when Father bought the place, but the crystal chandeliers, the woodwork and the decorative plasterwork on the ceiling were looking rather sad then. You've turned all this Wedgwood blue and cream and gold into something extremely lovely. Gideon's lucky to have found you, Caroline. To help him with this, I mean."

"I wish now I hadn't saved this room for last," Caroline said. "You could have had a better view of it if I'd finished."

"It looks almost perfect as it is," Erin said gently. "We'll help you."

"Oh no," Caroline insisted. "That's why Gideon hired me. It's my job."

Erin gave in graciously, glancing down at what Caroline had been looking at with such concentration when they came in.

"May I see what you're working on?"

Caroline held up an antique, off-the-shoulder ball gown of deep cream. Gideon remembered Erin once coming to him in tears because their mother had flown into a rage at her for touching a family heirloom. He had held his sister close, soothed her tears, and they had agreed then that they hated the heirlooms their mother worshipped. He knew Erin still resented them, just as he knew that Caroline's romantic soul was responsible for that dreamy look in her eyes as she gazed at the dress.

"These are yours and Gideon's," Caroline said softly, indicating the pile of formal clothing still tucked in the box. "I suppose some people would suggest you donate them to a museum and put them in a collection, but— wouldn't it be interesting to try them on? You'd look absolutely stunning in this Regency style, Erin," she said, holding up the creamy cloth.

Erin's eyes opened wide. She touched her hand to her throat in a gesture of nervousness. Gideon knew what she was thinking. No one, most especially his mother, had ever suggested actually putting any of these items to use. It was unthinkable. His mother would have called it a crime.

"You want me to *wear* the dress?" his sister asked in a soft, stilted voice.

In spite of her thirty-five years, for a moment, Gideon thought, she was a child again. A pretty, dark-haired child in awe of her mother's too precious treasures. A child who felt she mattered less than those treasures.

Caroline's hand stilled on the gown. "I'm sorry." She looked up at him, dark uncertainty coloring her blue eyes. "I suppose that was a bit irreverent of me. Excuse me. These are, as I said, your things, and they're valuable. Irreplaceable, really. I suppose it's just the drama teacher in me that escaped for a moment there.''

More likely the romantic woman who dwelled within her, Gideon thought, the one he shied away from and needed to protect from the man within himself who had no romance in his heart. Still, he felt for her now. She was uncomfortable and he remembered that first day when she'd told him she would feel out of place trying to entertain his sister. He saw now just what a burden he'd placed on her. She was afraid to be herself and he didn't know how to assure her that ''herself'' was just who she should be. He watched as she placed the gown back in the box. ''Would you like these stored somewhere special?'' she asked.

But Erin was watching Caroline closely, and Caroline's expression resembled Erin's own in the days before she realized that her mother valued these clothes more than she valued her daughter.

With a growing smile and a swift move, Erin picked up the gown. ''Caroline, I think you've hit on something here. Wearing this gown is a wonderful idea. In fact, why don't we get Sonia and Danielle and even Gideon, and we'll try on all these things? When we open the house for the party, we'll do it in style.''

A faint pink glow colored Caroline's cheeks. ''A sort of history pageant?'' she suggested carefully.

''Or a masked mini-ball,'' Erin said. ''We could share with the other guests. We're only having a small group and we still have a week. Gideon certainly has enough clout to employ tailors to fit everyone in that time.'' She looked down at the dress she still held and ran one hand over the lovely fabric. ''It *is* lovely, isn't it? I'd forgotten how beautiful my mother's things were. Thank you for helping me remember.''

When Erin had left to try on her treasure, Gideon smiled at Caroline. ''Still thinking of shrieking and fainting?'' he asked, reminding her of their conversation the day they'd first met.

She raised one brow. ''I'm too busy trying to remember all the rules I read in those books. Fainting will have to wait.''

He smiled at her gently. ''Thank you for making Erin's day. My mother never let her near these things.''

She shook her head. ''I can't take credit, since I was just being impetuous. It could have turned out all wrong. And thank *you* for helping me through yesterday. Do you think Erin knew we were doing more than getting a kite out of a tree?''

''I'm sure she didn't,'' he lied.

He could almost see the relief wash over Caroline's body. But she was still stiff, obviously on her guard. He wanted to go to her, place his hands on her shoulders, invite her to rest her head against his chest as he massaged the tension from her body. But that would be a mistake. This woman was getting under his skin way too much, and he just couldn't let that happen. He was as much a product of his parents as his sister was, and while some things might change, like Erin's realization that she could now touch her mother's collection without fear, other things never would. He was too old to learn how to love and to care deeply enough to please a wife and a child. Caroline had come into his life many decades too late. And he would not hurt her for the world.

''What?'' she asked, and he realized he was still staring at her.

"Nothing," he said with a forced smile.

"We'll manage," she said, and he knew she understood. Maybe she was right. They had come this far. All they had to do was survive the next seven days.

Surely that wouldn't be a problem.

Caroline was, as he had predicted, perfect at being a hostess, Gideon thought three days later. Only being right felt very wrong, he acknowledged, as he once again watched her smile graciously. For the last few days Caroline had been in the right place at the right time, had made suggestions for his guests' comfort, and had made sure that everyone was entertained. She was the perfect hostess. Erin would find no reason to worry about his care and comfort. *He* could find nothing at all to fault in Caroline's behavior.

Except that she wasn't being Caroline. Gone was the woman who had flown a kite, frolicked through his fountain, and raided his freezer at midnight. After that first day, she and Roy had kept Libby under wraps and the only traces he'd seen of the old Caroline, he was seeing right at this moment. And that was only because they had all traveled into town to visit the art fair on the green, and they had just run into Caroline's friends, Emily and Rebecca.

"Em. Becky," she called, giving her friends a warm hug. "You look great. You're doing well?" she asked, like a worried mother hen.

"I'm fine, except for missing you two," Emily said. "What do you say we all take a trip to San Francisco at the end of the summer. I'd love to get away…"

"Sounds like heaven," Rebecca agreed. "Just the three of us, the way it's always been."

At her friend's words, Caroline looked slightly more worried. "You're sure you're okay? Those men you're working for are treating you well?"

"I'm great," Emily agreed somewhat hesitantly. "The surprise party Simon and are giving for his aunt will soon be over and my job with him will be as well." Even Gideon picked up on the stress in her voice. He could almost feel concern rolling off Caroline, but he noticed she didn't pry.

Her friend Rebecca gave a small, tight nod. "I'm great. The grand opening of Logan's hotel is going well," she said, looking at her employer who was standing nearby. "My job with Logan won't last much longer, either. You're okay, too?"

Caroline's laugh was almost the old laugh he knew. "Oh, I'm always okay, Rebecca. And count me in on the vacation. Just the three of us. We can eat our way from one end of the city to the other and check out every street performer in town. Be wild, a little crazy. It'll be fun." And she smiled that brilliant, heart-melting smile, the one he'd missed. He knew in that moment that the stress of this job was more than he should have asked from her. She was holding her bubbly personality at bay. For him. Because she thought that was what he expected or that his guests would want, he realized, remembering her reluctance that first day they met. The thought ignited an anger deep inside him. At himself.

So when she said goodbye to her friends and returned to escorting Danielle and Sonia through the maze of local artists, he patted Erin's arm. "Be back in a moment, dear," he told her. "There's someone I need to talk to."

"Just when I've finally found a few minutes alone in

a crowd with you?'' Erin chided. ''Tell me, who were those people your Caroline was talking to?''

He raised one brow. ''Getting nosy, Erin? They're simply friends of hers.''

''They seemed concerned for her. Is there something you're not telling me about your relationship? You watch her constantly. She watches you, too, but not as obviously.''

Was he that transparent about his lust for Caroline? Apparently so. The thought annoyed him tremendously. He already knew that she was nervous about what his sister would think of her. If Erin even suspected that he dreamed about his beautiful assistant in his bed, Caroline would be mortified. And Erin might rightfully wonder if the past was going to repeat itself. He'd damn well better do more to hide his interest than he'd been doing so far.

''Caroline and I have been working together for over two weeks, Erin. We're both concentrating on making your visit a success.''

She frowned, opened her mouth, and then closed it again. He stared back at her silently. ''All right,'' she finally said. ''It *is* none of my business. You win. And as you said, you need to talk to someone right now. Business?''

He gave her a slight smile of thanks. ''Important business,'' he agreed. But it was Rebecca and Emily he eventually approached, finding them at last at a small table near the lemonade stand with Logan Brewster nearby. ''Ladies,'' he said, ''I'm—''

''The reason Caroline is looking pale?'' Emily asked.

''And tense?'' Rebecca demanded.

He sighed. ''Apparently so. She's taking this job as hostess to my guests very seriously.''

Rebecca stared back at him. Directly. Unfalteringly, as if she were sizing him up. "I'm sure she takes her job seriously. Caroline would. Still, I'm not sure what you've asked her to do, but Mr. Tremayne, do you really think your guests would object to Caroline being—well, Caroline? She's an absolute sweetheart, and it shows. She's completely caring."

"She's that," he acknowledged. "And I couldn't agree with you more about no one objecting to her being herself, but I wonder—she's worked so hard to perfect this image, this part—what will she do if I ask her to drop it?"

The two women exchanged glances. "I see what you mean," Emily answered. "Rejection city. No actress wants the critics panning her act. Least of all Caroline."

"Nevertheless," he continued, "I don't want her getting ill. I don't like to see her like this, even if she looks completely natural to the rest of the world."

"Then do something," Rebecca urged.

"I intend to. Any suggestions?"

"Get her off the stage," Emily suggested gently. "Just for awhile. She's really fine, you know. Caroline knows what she's doing. She lives this way. She lets loose for the kids, then puts on the professional face for teacher conferences and meetings. We all do, of course, but with Caroline, the difference is just a little more jolting, because she's so very alive. Still, she could probably stand a breather if she's been doing this nonstop for days."

"Off her stage?" Gideon said, considering. "That sounds workable. Possible. An interesting idea." He nodded to both of them. "Thank you, ladies."

"You're welcome, and—Mr. Tremayne?" Rebecca called, as he turned to walk away.

"Yes?"

"Be gentle. We wouldn't want to have to hurt you, but we would, if Caroline came home damaged in any way." The lady's tone was teasing, but there was a touch of honesty in her eyes.

"I agree with you completely," he said. "Anyone who would hurt Caroline would deserve a most cruel fate. I'd help you."

He wasn't teasing, about his concern for Caroline, or his gratitude for her friends' suggestion. They were right, he knew. She was acting. If he could just pull her behind the curtains for a few minutes, she could breathe. He darn well didn't want her completely submerging her own soul for his sake. Not for Erin's sake, either.

But, he found, as the day progressed, getting Caroline offstage wasn't all that easy. She seemed to have programmed herself to see to Erin, Danielle and Sonia's needs. If Sonia expressed an interest in shellfish, Caroline was off to the kitchen to confer with Mrs. Williams. When Erin mentioned the local shops, Caroline organized an expedition. Only one thing seemed to slow her down, only one person, and that was the person Gideon had been avoiding for days on end.

Which was why he found himself climbing the stairs to Libby's room late that afternoon.

"She needs a breather," he reminded himself, taking the steps slowly. "She'll be gone in a few days and have a lifetime of living without this. But I won't be there. I won't get a chance to see her back in her element." And therein lay the real truth. He did want Caroline to feel at home, to be her own comfortable self, but maybe even more than that, he just plain missed the woman's natural warmth.

And knowing that, he should turn around, let things play out to their inevitable end.

He kept climbing, knocked lightly on Libby's door and entered. The child, he could see, was asleep in her crib. And Caroline was seated in a wing chair. Her shoes were off, her stockinged feet pulled up beneath her. She was still wearing the long khaki skirt she'd had on this morning and the white blouse, but she'd pulled her hair from the pins which had been imprisoning it not long ago, and it fell over her shoulders brushing the curves of her breasts. She'd unfastened the top two buttons of her blouse, and pushed the sleeves up to her elbows. She was holding a core of an apple and a book was sliding off her lap as she looked up, wide-eyed, and attempted to hurriedly begin to put herself back together.

"Don't," he said softly, as she reached for the gaping placket of her blouse. "Just—don't. Please," he continued, letting his voice drop even lower, as he moved to her side and smiled down into her eyes. "If you attempt to fasten even one button, Caroline, or put your hair back into that tight little knot you've been wearing, I'm going to have to get down on my knees and beg you not to. That could prove very humiliating, but I would do it."

"Gideon?" she said, in a soft, somewhat small voice. "I—I guess I lost track of the time. I should have been downstairs already," and she started to rise.

As if he'd thought the woman would listen to reason when she felt she had a responsibility to attend to. After all, this was Caroline, and she was as stubborn as she was good.

The word "stubborn" made him smile. At least here was a trace of the lady he'd been seeking.

He dropped to his knees beside her chair. "I warned you," he told her.

"Gideon, what are you doing?"

Ah, now he had her attention completely. At last. Her blue eyes were wide and filled with uncertainty. He wanted nothing more than to catch her face between his palms, lower his lips to hers as he gazed into those eyes, and make a connection with this woman.

"I'm here to ask you to take a few hours off to recharge your engine," he said. "Actually, as your employer, I'm demanding that you do so. You need more than short snatches of time to yourself."

"I'm fine," she said firmly. "Perfectly fine." She sat up straighter, and pulled her legs from beneath her. The book she'd been reading slid to the floor with a thud. They both reached down for it, and his fingers brushed against hers.

The heat that slipped through him was immediate, sudden, consuming. She raised her head, looked into his eyes, her lips the merest whisper away from his own.

"I've missed you, lady," he told her then. "Damn, I've missed you."

She bit down on her lip.

He groaned.

"I'm here, Gideon," she whispered. "I've always been here."

"Not good enough," he said. "Not close enough."

He placed his hands on her arms, pulled her straight off her perch into his arms, onto his lap. He gathered her close, plunged the fingers of his left hand into the silk of her curls and brought his lips down on hers.

It was like tipping a candle's flame to an acre of parched tinder. She turned molten in his arms. Twisting, her hands twining about his neck, her lips returning kiss for kiss. She arched closer, filled the small space between them, her breasts crushing against his chest.

"I didn't want to do this," she whispered harshly when he let her up for a short gasp of air.

"No. I know," he agreed as she nipped back in for another taste. He trailed kisses down over her lips, the delicate line of her jaw, down her throat to that delicious space she'd opened to him by unbuttoning those buttons. He nudged yet another button aside.

"I'm sorry. I know I shouldn't be touching you," he murmured. "I'll stop in a minute."

"Yes, but not just yet. In a minute," she said, pushing closer, placing her hands at the neckline of his shirt and pulling, popping the buttons on his shirt and following the trail with her own lips. "In just one minute."

Then he found her lips again. The taste of her filled his senses, and he knew he'd never, ever forget the sweet, heady flavor of her. She was unique. She was Caroline. And he was going to have just a bit more of her before he let her go.

Except, suddenly, he heard the sound of Libby's first waking movements as the baby turned in her crib.

Except the door to Caroline's room was opening. He opened his eyes, and looked up—right into Erin's speculative smile.

Immediately he pulled Caroline closer, frowning at his sister.

She got the idea and quickly stepped back outside and shut the door.

But not before Caroline turned her head and saw her.

He felt the gasp move through her body as she twisted and struggled to her feet. He followed her up, saw how her hands were shaking as she tried to fasten the buttons at her throat, as she looked wildly around toward the door. Erin was already gone, but the damage had been done.

"What must she have been thinking?" Caroline whispered, pulling her sleeves down, smoothing out the wrinkles in her skirt. "That I would be here kissing you, my employer. Oh Gideon."

Immediately he reached out for her, intending to—do what? To kiss her again? No, to comfort, to tell her everything was all right, but then it wasn't, was it? Nothing was all right. History was repeating itself in the worst way.

"This was my fault, Caroline. All mine."

"No." Caroline continued her attempts to put her clothing in order.

"Yes," he insisted, giving up on not touching her. He placed his palms on her forearms, and stilled her movements. "I came here looking for you, and whether I realized it or not at the time, Caroline, I came here to do exactly what I did. I'd been wanting to kiss you again, and I did. You, if you recall, were here minding your own business, reading your book," he added, picking it up and returning it to her.

"Gideon, I ripped the buttons off your shirt."

He smiled at that, even though there was little to smile about. He had come here and taken when he had nothing real or lasting to offer. The fact that he had also put Caroline in an embarrassing position was ripping through him. He had been very much aware of what he was doing while he was doing it, and a part of him

wished his sister had held off a bit longer before inter-
rupting. Thinking that way was unforgivable. Crazy. All
the things he'd promised himself he wouldn't do or become.

Still, he didn't want Caroline standing here before him
thinking that way. She was in no way to blame for this
situation. He, of all people, had known what he was
about, and he had failed to heed the warnings. Now it
was up to him to set things right. That did not include
letting Caroline feel guilty about the last few minutes.

"I never liked this shirt much, anyway," he said.

She frowned, and poked him on the chest.

"I know what you're doing, Gideon," she told him.
"Well, it won't work. I get my share of the blame, too."

Okay, he'd humor her. In theory.

"All right," he said softly.

"Just that? Just 'all right'?"

"All right, I'll get someone to sew the buttons back
on my shirt if it bothers you that badly."

She opened her eyes wide and crossed her arms. "You
most certainly will not. You give me that shirt and let
me repair it. I don't want anyone else knowing that I
was—that I was—"

"Delectable?"

"—that I was half undressed and devouring you in
front of your sister, Gideon," she said in a rather small
voice. "We were well on the way to something more.
That's nothing to joke about."

He ran his hands up her arms, tipped her toward him
and dropped a swift kiss on the top of her head. "Erin
and I are close. I'll talk to her. I'll explain."

"And what will you tell her?"

He held out his hands palm up. He shook his head.

"The truth. That there's a mutual attraction between us, but that we're fighting it—most of the time. That we don't have a relationship. That we'd both been feeling the stress of being on company manners these last few days and I had sought you out to talk to you for a bit of rest and relaxation. It's true, you know. I didn't know I would kiss you when I came up here. I only meant to spend a little restful time in your company."

She looked up at him then and smiled, shaking her head. "You're a strange man, Gideon. Most people don't find me exactly restful."

"Most people must be idiots, then, but I'll leave you to your book now, Caroline." He looked down at the title. *The Knighthood in History*. A picture of a bold male in full armor perched on a midnight destrier graced the cover.

"It's not at all what you're thinking, not even vaguely romantic," she insisted, even though he hadn't said a thing. "I wanted to do some research on your family history. Your sister has shown an interest."

He simply nodded. "Then enjoy, Caroline," he said. He turned to the baby who had awakened and was standing up in her crib, gooing and rocking back and forth, reaching out with her little hands as if he were a new stuffed animal she'd just discovered and had to have.

He indulged himself by allowing himself to wink at her. She obligingly cooed. A soft, trusting little sound. A trickle of warmth went through him at the sound, followed by a spear of regret. Libby and Caroline. Both innocents, both people he could harm if he didn't watch himself much more closely. He silently blessed the baby for being such a visible reminder of that.

"Caroline," he said carefully, as he placed his hand

on the doorknob. "Just don't feel you and Libby have to hide up here, all right? You don't have to lock yourself away in order to be yourself. Erin's my sister, not my keeper."

"And we're supposed to be reassuring her, not making her wonder whether every woman in your employ has designs on you."

"Don't worry about that. I'll tell her you don't. That you're looking for a different kind of man."

She blinked, and then stared at him. "Good. I'd want her to know that."

A sliver of something decidedly sharp and painful lanced through him. Guilt, probably, he surmised. He hoped.

"Then she *will* know it. This is not going to amount to anything, Caroline. All right?"

She nodded slowly.

Somehow he managed to smile. "Be yourself, Caroline. Share your smile, and your laughter, too, if you would. It brightens the day. I'm sure my sister and her friends will appreciate you even more if you'll just be you."

She looked uncertain.

"And if you do that," he added, "I'll be less tempted to climb the stairs to reassure myself that you're all right."

She drew in a shuddery breath. "Then I guess it would be best if I opened up a little," she agreed.

"Thank you," he said, and shut the door behind him. But he didn't really feel that he'd accomplished what he'd wanted to. What he'd done, he was almost certain, was take her one haven, the place where she felt free to let loose, and turn it into a place where she'd been embarrassed. She'd been caught kissing a man who'd made it clear that when he kissed a woman, he was just looking for a temporary amusement. He intended to make sure he didn't harm her in that way again.

Chapter Nine

All right, this looked bad, Caroline admitted to herself after Gideon had gone. She'd been caught going wild in the man's arms, and she was pretty sure he really wasn't going to let her take any of the blame in spite of what he'd said. Right now he was probably telling his sister that he was his father come back to life when, heaven knew, she had practically jumped into his arms. He'd cover for her because Gideon had a thing about protecting women and children. Hadn't he done his best to smooth things over for Paula when she'd left here?

So she'd just have to be the one to tell Erin that *she'd* been just as much to blame for losing her head as he had. *And* admit to herself that she was doing a rotten job of staying emotionally uninvolved with Gideon.

"But first, Erin," Caroline said, marching down the hall to deliver Libby to Roy and make sure that the two of them had everything they needed. "The woman needs to know the facts."

But that was easier said than done, she realized when she finally located Erin on the patio a full twenty minutes after the incident with Gideon. How could she tactfully confess she was physically a fool for the lady's brother?

"You wanted to talk to me?" Erin said, slipping her sunglasses off as Caroline moved nearer. "About Gideon, I'm guessing. He's something, isn't he?"

Caroline hoped the heat in her cheeks was only due to the sun. "He's an excellent employer, and I—I wanted to explain."

Erin rose. "Don't worry," she said in a soft, soothing voice. "Gideon already talked to me."

"He told you it was all his fault, didn't he?"

"Of course," Erin said, smiling. "That's Gideon."

"But he'd be wrong on this count. I mean, that is…"

"You mean it takes two to complete a scorcher of an embrace like that?" Erin looked up expectantly.

Caroline opened her eyes wide. "Yes, I guess that's exactly what I'm saying. But I want you to know that it—"

"Didn't mean anything?"

"Yes. I mean, no. It most certainly did mean something, but only that I'm attracted to your brother. I don't want you to think that I have any designs on him. None at all."

"So if he asked you to marry him, you'd tell him to hit the road?"

"He wouldn't do that."

"But if he did?"

"He wouldn't. And I wouldn't. We've both agreed it's not what we want. So even if I find your brother—"

"Hotter than the center of the earth?"

Caroline blinked at the woman's tendency to finish

her sentences. "Even if I find Gideon very appealing, that's as far as it goes, or will go."

"Because you don't want him?"

"We're just not right together."

"And you came to tell me that because you were worried that I'd think less of you because you kissed Gideon."

Caroline took a few seconds to think about that comment. "I suppose that's partly true—I generally don't want people to think badly of me. But mostly I came because I knew that Gideon was going to take the blame, and I wanted you to know that he's been very good to me, he's treated me with respect and care. He hasn't offered me anything improper."

"Except for that kiss."

"Which wasn't forced on me. Gideon wouldn't do that."

Erin rose to her feet. She took Caroline's hands in her own. "Then, thank you."

Caroline stared into the earnest gray eyes of the other woman.

"For what? I can't imagine what you must be thinking."

"I'm thinking that you understand Gideon. After the way our father carried on, Gideon feels a tremendous responsibility for those who live under his roof. Thank you for realizing he would never intentionally hurt you—and for being brave enough to approach me. No one's ever been there to stand up for Gideon before. You're a woman I'd want for a sister, you know."

A sense of warmth spread through Caroline, but also a sense of panic. "Gideon's lucky to have a sister who cares as much as you do, but I have to be honest here.

Nothing's going to happen between your brother and me, Erin. That is, I can't promise I won't kiss him again. I seem to have a weakness in that direction, but beyond that, this is a dead-end street.''

Erin smiled. ''You're right, I'm sure. You and Gideon have discussed this. I guess I was just in the mood for good news. Forgive me for pushing.''

Caroline shook her head. ''There's nothing to forgive. I have siblings, too. I understand about wanting to make things work for them, but I'm glad you can see that nothing's going to happen between Gideon and me.''

''Yes, I'm glad you shared that with me,'' Erin said with a broader smile. ''This talk has been most... enlightening.''

''She was worried that I'd think badly of you,'' Erin confided to her brother a short time later. ''I think you've picked a very special lady to help you, Gideon.''

''Caroline is like no other,'' Gideon agreed.

''Does she know you feel that way?''

He carefully studied his sister. ''She knows I appreciate the job she's doing, yes.''

''Does she know you appreciate her as a woman?''

Gideon frowned. ''I love you, Erin, but you're overstepping the bounds of sisterly love. I only discussed Caroline with you earlier because I knew she'd be concerned and because I didn't want any misunderstanding about her.''

''I don't think I've misunderstood. She's special—and she has a hold on your emotions, doesn't she?''

''There's nothing—'' he began, until Erin raised her brows. ''All right, there is something, but nothing that's going to come to anything. I've had many women, little sister, but never for long. Caroline is not a woman that a man takes on for a few months and then sets aside. Do you understand?''

''Yes. You're going to stamp out any hope of a relationship.''

''The relationship wouldn't have lasted. Mine don't. They can't. It's just not the way I operate, and frankly, it's best this way. Do you understand that, too?''

He knew she did, because there were tears in her eyes. ''I understand that you've chosen a solitary life because of things that were beyond your control and I hate that.''

He smiled gently and dried her tears. ''It's the best life for me, Erin. Really. We're different, you and I. You want things that I have never desired, and this life of mine has always worked for me. This is the way I want things. Really.''

But in the days that followed, Gideon realized his sister hadn't given up as easily as he'd thought. Every time he turned around, Erin was inviting him on an expedition with her friends and Caroline. The two of them were being ''studied,'' which was the best word he could come up with. And all this enforced togetherness with Caroline was intolerable, given that he was trying his best not to touch her again. He didn't want her worrying about Erin's reactions, and he didn't want her hurt. Being with her in a group where she was close and yet completely out of range was exquisite torture. He finally elected to tell her so when he caught her alone in the kitchen one morning.

''This has got to stop, Caroline. Erin is doing it again.''

"I know. She loves you and thinks being with me will make you happy."

"It does make me happy. You know I enjoy your company, but—"

"But not like this," Caroline agreed. "Not when we're being watched constantly. I feel like everyone's gauging our reactions to each other. Like those animals in the zoo that they've decided to mate."

Gideon sucked in a deep breath. He turned fierce eyes on her.

"Sorry," she said quickly. "Maybe that wasn't exactly the best analogy."

"It was a perfect analogy," he admitted. "But like most of those animals, I presume, I prefer to do my mating in private."

She gave him a long, assessing glance. And then she smiled.

He smiled back. "Okay, we've both agreed we're not going to go down that road, but this matchmaking is making us both crazy. If I have to smile politely at you under the watchful eyes of Erin, while she tries to measure every look we share, I'm going to start pulling out my hair."

"Don't. It's gorgeous hair," she teased. "And yes, I agree, it's torture. Not only that, but I'm feeling very sorry for Sonia. She really wants you badly, Tremayne. I have to say that you're showing admirable restraint. A whole bevy of women who find you sexy as hell and a sister who is hoping you'll jump at the bait being offered."

"And you're being amazingly patient with that sister," he said softly. "Thank you. She needs this, I think, right now, while she's still recovering from a painful relationship. I'd like to think all this managing of you and me is helping her.''

"I like her," Caroline admitted. "She's a loyal sister, and a genuinely good person."

"But you need a day off. You've devoted so much of your time and energy planning tomorrow's party and to impressing my sister, that you've got to be stressed," Gideon decided. "Let's give you some time to just kick back."

"No, I can't. There are only two days left before everyone, including me, leaves anyway, and Sonia wants to go to the matinee they're showing at the dinner theater."

"And she will, along with Erin and Danielle. I'll order a limo for them. As for you and me—we're down to our last two days, too, and I have other plans, thanks to Roy."

"Roy?"

Gideon grinned. "Roy informed me two days ago that I should really visit the White Thunder Waterslide Park before I die. Somehow I think the young man is of the opinion that I'm in danger of meeting my demise any day now, being as ancient as I am. I suspect he plans to take care of you when I go, but in the meantime, he has graciously agreed to help you, me and…the baby sneak out today. After the festivities begin tomorrow night, we won't have any more time together."

For a moment, he thought she caught her breath. For just a second he thought he saw a trace of regret in her eyes, but then she raised both brows, staring at his customary white shirt, tie and black pants. He could almost see the "Caroline" wheels turning in her head. He was not exactly prone to dressing for down and dirty and wet.

"A waterslide? Do you know what you're doing, Gideon?"

"If you mean, have I been to a waterslide, no, I haven't. If you mean, am I aware that I'm about to kidnap a woman and a child to ensure that we all have a day of fun before we go completely crazy, I'm very much of sound mind, Caroline."

"And you're sure this is what you want to do? How you want to spend your day?"

"I'm sure I want to get you out and away from watchful eyes so you can laugh and be yourself for a few hours, yes."

"Then allow me to follow you to your doom, Gideon. I'll just go get—"

"—the baby," they said together.

Caroline had only been to the White Thunder Waterslide Park one time before, and it was still as much a wonder to behold the second time around. With more than a dozen tubes and slides, a wave pool, a tubing run, a sand beach, and a wading pool, it was the perfect place to be on a hot summer day. And with Roy and his main woman of the week along for the ride, there were plenty of adults available to take turns entertaining Libby.

"Are you having fun yet?" she laughingly asked Gideon as he spun out of a long slide and hit the water beneath.

"I'll have to give Roy a raise," he said with a slow smile, shoving his hands through his hair. Droplets sluiced down his chest and continued on toward the waistband of a pair of black trunks, making Caroline feel suddenly warmer than the day merited. "And yes, I'm having fun," he agreed. "My mother would have called this slumming with the commoners. I like it. You're introducing me to all kinds of things, Caroline."

Caroline tried not to notice the way those long wet lashes framed his deep gray eyes. She told herself that today wasn't really special even if it felt that way. This was the beginning of goodbye. She needed to remember that and to start thinking about her tomorrows, the plans she'd spent a lifetime forming.

"This was Roy's idea, not mine," she said.

"Yes, but Roy told me that you'd been thinking about taking Libby here. I wouldn't have come otherwise."

It was the mention of Libby that finally enabled Caroline to smile and pull back from the turbulent feelings flitting through her.

"I should find Libby," she said. "Roy and his girlfriend deserve some fun, too. You can stay," she said when he started to follow her.

He shook his head. "This day was meant as an escape for you," he insisted. "And you might need help juggling all that equipment you've brought."

"Babies *do* necessitate a truckload of supplies," she said, with a laugh. Then after she had located Roy and sent him off to frolic with his lady she settled on a chaise lounge in the sandy area next to the wading pool. Picking up Libby, Caroline reached into the huge diaper bag she'd brought, and pulled out a small container of crackers.

But Libby fussed, whimpering when Caroline tried to give her something to drink. She offered the child her favorite stuffed tiger. Still no luck.

"Is she all right?" Gideon asked stiffly as the baby

raised sad eyes to him and climbed off Caroline's lap onto the sand.

"She's just tired, poor baby," Caroline said. "I should take her home, but it doesn't seem fair to Roy when he hasn't had much time in the water yet. I'll try to get her to sleep. Come here, love," she said.

"Noooo," Libby wailed when Caroline tried to lift her. She didn't raise her face for her usual kiss. Instead she latched onto Gideon's chaise lounge. She looked up at him with wide, blue, tear-filled eyes. She raised her tiny arms.

He looked down.

"I'll take her," Caroline said quickly, as Libby let out a piteous wail. "When she's tired, she gets stubborn."

"Like you," Gideon said softly and scooped the baby up onto his chest. Immediately she nestled there. Caroline could see him tense. For long seconds he kept his hands stiffly at his sides. Then he placed one big palm on the baby's back to hold her steady and keep her secure.

"I'll—I'll take her," Caroline repeated, starting to rise.

"It's all right," he said carefully. "It's only just this once. And since she's already here, well, it's one thing to choose not to have children, Caroline. It's another to reject a child who's already here. She's tired," he said, repeating Caroline's words. "She's fine. For now."

But though his hand rested gently on the baby's back, though his fingers strayed to her tousled curls now and again, Caroline could see that Gideon never really relaxed the whole time that Libby lay sleeping in his arms. He didn't want a baby to feel rejection.

She wondered again what awful things had happened during his childhood. And she realized once and for all, that this man would never seek parenthood. He might hold a child who needed holding when there was no alternative, but he wouldn't choose that kind of closeness and responsibility for himself, and she would do well to remember that.

The little girl stirred in his arms and Gideon shifted, trying to make her more comfortable. She yawned widely, rubbing her fists in her eyes. Then she blinked, yawned again, and then pulled to her knees, staring him straight in the face.

He couldn't help it then. He smiled. "Had enough snooze time, Princess?"

She answered by squealing with delight and planting her palms on his cheeks. She bent closer, apparently curious about this adult who'd finally spoken to her.

He noted that her silky blond curls had sprung up from where they'd been crushed against his chest.

"Hey, Libby," he whispered. "Want to surprise Aunt Caroline?" He looked across the foot of space that separated his chair from Caroline's. The lady had fallen asleep in the sun, one long strand of auburn hair catching on the moist fullness of her lips, another curl coiling across the slim white strap of her bathing suit. She was so beautiful in sleep, her lashes resting on the cream of her skin, her long, luscious limbs relaxed. She shifted at his whisper and Gideon sucked in a deep breath as she turned on her side, giving him a delightful if forbidden view of the lovely slopes of her breasts.

"Yes, I'd say that you and I had better make ourselves

busy,'' he said to the little girl whose sweet baby scent mingled with the coconut smell of suntan oil.

He lowered her to the ground, stood and took her hand. Together they walked the few feet to where Libby's pail and shovel were lying.

''Your Aunt Caroline likes castles. Let's make her a castle, all right?''

The little girl nodded and smiled boldly back at him. She squatted in the sand, gazing at his work worshipfully as he shaped the sand. Now and then, she would pat at it, stick her shovel in the structure and send it tumbling. A gurgling little giggle would follow.

Gideon leveled a long look at her from beneath his brows. ''We'll never get this done if you keep doing that, angelface.''

But she only seemed more delighted at his mock-stern look. She clapped her hands and crept closer. As he worked, she reached down and picked up a tiny handful of wet sand and presented it to him.

''Thank you, love,'' he said, taking her offering, but when he looked down, she was staring up at him, her little lips puckered.

He couldn't *not* kiss her. He couldn't reject her very precious gift.

Gently he leaned his cheek close for her to kiss. He felt the tiny smacking against the roughness of his skin. He turned and received the smile he knew she'd offer then.

What a precious little thing she was. How could anyone not want her?

But the baby's father didn't want her, Caroline had said.

And he himself didn't. Not really. Oh yes, he was

enjoying this moment, but even his parents had occasionally enjoyed him in those moments when they were in an unusually good mood. As he was today.

"So enjoy the day, Tremayne," he told himself. "It's a gift, but tomorrow will come, sooner or later." And both Caroline and this little sweetheart would soon be gone.

The thought had been nagging him, sharp and stinging for days. But he knew the stinging would soon stop. This situation had been unusual, so of course he'd gotten caught up in things. Still, once he made it through his last moments with Caroline, life would return to normal. And then, maybe, he could finally stop wanting and worrying about this woman.

Chapter Ten

The night of the party, Caroline stared in the mirror and realized that she really *did* look like she was back on stage. The dress she'd chosen from the Tremayne collection was ice blue with a low-cut fitted bodice, short puffed sleeves, and a skirt that swept the toes of her shoes. Her hair was pulled back and fell in loose waves over her shoulders. She looked like a lady from another era, but deep inside she was still Caroline. And it was her last night with Gideon, she thought, feeling ragged panic rise within her.

She hadn't been prepared for just how difficult this goodbye would be, but then she hadn't thought she'd let herself get involved, either. She shouldn't have. It was crazy, absolutely hopeless, and besides, it was wrong. Gideon would be devastated if he knew she was going to miss him so much.

"So he won't," she whispered. "So let's pretend. Just one more time." She swept out the door and down the stairs. By tomorrow evening she would be gone, leaving only a freezer full of ice cream. Everyone else would have left as well. Gideon would have his life back. That had always been the plan.

But she couldn't think about that now. A dozen guests would soon be arriving. She still had a role to play tonight and she wasn't sure she'd really convinced Erin that Gideon was doing fine on his own.

When she got to the bottom of the stairs, he was there, stealing her breath, more so than usual. Gideon was always gorgeous, he always made her nerves sing just by looking at her, but in formal black and white, he made her very heart stop beating.

Somehow, she said her hellos and moved on. They met again briefly as they welcomed their guests. He smiled and complimented her on the flowers in the ballroom, and she smiled back just as politely, but they were like wooden people. On display. They had a job to do.

They were doing it well, she decided a half-hour later. Their guests had entered into the spirit of the ball wholeheartedly. There was a colorful swirl of lords and ladies gracing the mansion.

"All right, you can start breathing again, Caroline," a low, deep voice said behind her. She turned to find Gideon standing there. So close. His soap and aftershave and all-male scent drifted to her. Despite his words, she inhaled deeply and held her breath, just for a second or two. To hold a part of him close.

"Everyone's enjoying themselves," he assured her.

"You too? Are you taking time to smell the orchids, Mr. Tremayne?" she teased.

"Me too," he said with a grin. "Absolutely. Your

ball is perfect, Caroline, so you can stop shifting from one foot to the other.''

She did just that. She took another deep breath and smiled back, removing her half-mask. ''It *is* working, isn't it?''

He chuckled. ''I'll bet you say that in the middle of every play you put on.''

''Only ninety-eight percent of them. We do have a few disasters now and then. People forget their lines. Scenery topples on the players. Sometimes.''

''Not this time,'' he said. ''You've scored a coup, Ms. O'Donald,'' he said. ''Allow me to congratulate you.'' He took her hand in his own. He played the game and bowed over her fingertips and let his lips brush against her skin. The merest whisper of contact. She felt the swirl of want trickle in, slowly at first, then faster, more fiercely as he glanced up at her. He still held her hand, and his eyes were dark, with an underlying trace of— something.

In an instant, he'd banished the look and released her.

''You're lovely tonight, Caroline.'' His forced smile snapped her heart in half, but she managed to smile back.

''You're looking dark and handsome yourself, Gideon. But you *are* making my job more difficult. If Erin thinks you're a target for unscrupulous women, she might worry.''

''She's smiling,'' Gideon noted. ''I've missed her smile. Thank you, Caroline. You've made her happy these last few days, I think. She tells me you've made her laugh.''

A guest wandered near just then. Caroline moved closer for the sake of privacy. ''Erin was made to laugh,'' she said softly. ''She'd just forgotten how, for awhile. And I'd say that much of her happiness, most of it, has simply come from being in the company of the brother she's missed.''

He tilted his head. ''All right, we'll both take the credit. What's important is that Erin is recovering.''

Indeed, the lady was dancing right this minute with Roy who had gotten into the spirit of the party the moment he'd arrived. Her creamy skirts swirled as Roy swung her close.

Gideon frowned. ''That boy is a flirt and he's—''

Caroline placed her hand lightly on the muscles tensing beneath Gideon's sleeve. ''Gideon, Roy's dancing with everyone. And Erin's not taking him seriously. She's not in danger of being hurt by him,'' she said gently. ''In fact, if I'm not mistaken, she seems to have captured the attention of Brandon Hill.'' Caroline nodded in the direction of a man in his mid-thirties dressed all in black. The man was tall and lean and hawkish.

Gideon studied the man closely. ''You know him?''

She hesitated, but only for a second. ''Yes. He was a neighbor when I lived at home. He's very successful.''

''At what?''

The slightly suspicious tone of his voice had her smiling, but when she looked up at him he wasn't exactly smiling back. ''At running a newspaper, among other things.''

''How well do you know him?''

She blinked. ''You're wondering if he'll hurt Erin?''

''Actually,'' he said, sliding one hand around her waist and moving out onto the dance floor with her. ''I'm wondering if he's one of those men who hurt you in the past.''

She took a deep breath. "Brandon's a good guy," she promised him.

"So—he never kissed you?"

She caught her breath, stumbled slightly, but Gideon swung her close, gathered her up against the hardness of his chest, until she had her feet back beneath her. He did not loosen his hold once she'd recovered, and Caroline realized that her lips were dangerously close to his.

"He *did* kiss you?" he asked again, rephrasing the question.

This time she was able to smile. "Once. At a party. We were playing spin the bottle," she confided. "Brandon spun. He kissed me, but he did it because he had a terrible crush on my sister, Julie. I knew he did, and that she didn't know he was alive. So I went along, and Julie finally noticed him. They dated through high school. He's a nice man, Gideon. Julie would tell you so if she were here. They're still friends."

She finally felt him relax a bit. "And your sister didn't mind that you showed the man the moon and the stars that day."

"I didn't."

"You kissed him."

"It was all show."

"For you."

"For him, too."

Gideon chuckled. He swept her around the floor, his body brushing against hers. "Caroline, you amaze me. I've had your luscious lips beneath mine, and I can't imagine any male kissing you, even one who fancies himself in love with your sister, and not wanting to do it again."

"Thank you, I think," she said, as the music ended

and Gideon cruised her to a stop. ''But it was all very platonic, I assure you.'' She shrugged, and the low neckline of her dress slipped a quarter of an inch.

Gideon sucked in his breath. His eyes narrowed. He swept his hands up her arms and tugged the dress higher. ''All the same, I'm glad we're not playing spin the bottle tonight. If your Brandon is trying to get Erin's attention, I don't want him using you to do it. I don't want anyone using you.''

Including himself, his tone implied. Soon after that, Gideon took himself off. To play the host, he had said, and it was true, Caroline knew. But she also knew that he was putting some distance between them. He was protecting her from himself again. If he knew how easily he could hurt her, he'd be even more worried, and the last thing she wanted to bring to Gideon was worry. He spent too much time looking out for other people's happiness. Like Paula and Erin and Libby. Mrs. Williams. And yes, even herself.

So she followed Gideon's lead. She danced. She ate. She went out of her way to be entertaining and to do the job he had hired her to do. She wanted to help him, and so she put every ounce of effort into this last performance.

''You did it,'' Erin told her when their paths crossed a few minutes later. ''You brought the house to life, and you turned this ballroom into an absolute fantasy tonight. It's lovely. Magical. The most fun I've had in months. It feels like something's finally let loose inside me.''

''He's a nice man, Erin,'' Caroline said, nodding toward Brandon who had agreed to dance with Sonia and let Erin have a rest. ''A kind and peaceful man.''

"He is. Very. Thank you for inviting him. And I don't want you to think I'm ungrateful, but—"

"You're not ready yet."

"No," Erin said. "Not yet. I want to. I hope he'll still be here when I *am* ready, but not yet. Still, I wish I could show you how much I've valued your company this past week. You've been a friend to me and Danielle and Sonia, and I don't think it's just because Gideon hired you."

Caroline shook her head. "I like you. How could I not? You're a very good sister to Gideon."

"And family is very important to you. Gideon tells me you want a large one."

Caroline shrugged. "It's what I've always wanted."

"And what Gideon won't risk having." Erin sighed. "All right, so maybe you're not right for each other, but you've made him laugh while I've been here. And I'm not gone yet. There's still a little more time. For you. *And* for me," she said, turning purposefully toward Brandon.

"Gideon needs to laugh now and then, Caroline," she added. "He's done far too little of that in his life. Seeing him smile is important to me. It's why I came here. To make sure he was taking care of himself—that he was still capable of smiling in spite of having taken on the responsibility for the family fortune and name. I guess he is fine on his own, and so I suppose I'll do as he asks and go home. But before I go, I want him to see a little magic. That's what nights like this are for," she said, pointing toward the open doors leading to the balcony where the stars sparkled clear and bright.

When midnight rolled around, Caroline realized just what Erin had meant. She was dancing with Gideon, and one by one, their guests cut in, excusing themselves, and bidding the two of them goodnight. Like the stars at dawn, everyone faded away and soon Caroline was alone with Gideon.

"It's quiet," she said, realizing the music had stopped.

"Very," he said, still swaying with her in his arms.

"We can stop dancing now," she whispered, smiling against his shoulder.

"No. We can't."

She looked up into his eyes, dark and liquid in the moonlight sifting through the windows.

"We can't?"

"No, we can't. If we stop moving we'll have to deal with the fact that I suspect my sister has set us up. I saw her step through the door a moment ago. She locked it behind her."

"Erin?"

He laughed. "Erin likes to manage things. She always did. And if people didn't like to let her manage, she always found a way to help them along anyway."

"What do you think she expects us to do here?"

"What we're doing right now. Dealing with the chemistry."

"Gideon?" Caroline knew her voice was quivery, but she couldn't help it.

At the strained sound of her voice, he pulled her slightly closer, shaping his palm to her back. "Yes? Are you all right?"

She nodded. Hard. And felt the tightening of her body as the full reality of their situation became clear. She was alone in the dark with Gideon. In a quiet house. Nowhere to go, no way to back away from her thoughts.

"It's just—I'm not exactly dealing with the chemistry," she managed to say.

Immediately his hands loosened on her. "There's a way out. There's always a way out. Erin's heart is too soft to put us in a position where there are no options. She just wants to make it easier for us to choose the option she favors. In this case, she's made it very simple. The outside doors are open. See? We'll leave. I'll get you back to your own room," he whispered.

But suddenly the thought of going back to her room made her very sad. She would be leaving tomorrow afternoon. Her job was over. The fantasy had played out. Everyone was satisfied with the results. But she—she had an emptiness inside, a void.

It just wasn't possible to make those wise choices sometimes, she finally realized and accepted. Life chose for you. And in her case, life chose love. A love she couldn't have, it was true, but love, nonetheless. There was no point in fighting it. She knew that, knew she had always wanted love, waited for love, in spite of trying her best to run from it. And here it was, right in her path. She couldn't have this man forever. There was only one night left. For magic, Erin had said. And just a little magic at that. Just a kiss or two, so that he wouldn't feel he'd taken advantage. So that he would remember her with a smile. With fondness.

He was holding out his hand to her, to lead her back to her room.

She placed her hand in his. And then she stepped close, right in next to his heart. She rose up on her toes and placed her lips near his ear.

"Kiss me, Gideon."

He leaned her back in his arms, looked directly into

her eyes. ''I don't want to do anything that you'd regret.''

She smiled up at him. ''Then take me back to my room, Gideon. Deliver me safely home. But kiss me first. Once. Or twice. Or maybe a dozen times. Tomorrow isn't here yet, and tonight I'm another someone from another time,'' she said, indicating her gown with a sweep of her hand. ''So are you. Tomorrow we'll be Gideon and Caroline, employer and employee, with no regrets between us. But tonight—''

''Tonight there's only us,'' he said hoarsely. And he lifted her in his arms, folded her close, and covered her mouth with his own.

Once.

Twice.

A dozen times.

The stairs in his house seemed endlessly long, Gideon decided, as he descended to breakfast the next morning. For a moment last night, he'd stepped out of his skin, out of his soul and mated his mouth to Caroline's. He'd swept his hands over her body, several times, just enough to make him want more, just enough so that he'd still been able to stop.

He'd never have that mouth again. He'd never feel his hands on her. And he'd never after today, hear that laughter that made him think of life, full and round and so very warm.

But you've done the right thing, he thought. *You're doing the right thing in letting everything take its natural course and drift away today.*

And he would continue to do so for the rest of the day if he was wise. The muffled sound of packing was going on around him. His sister. Her friends. Caroline and Libby. Caroline would be having a tough time packing up all her things and taking care of a baby today, since Roy had taken up an offer to spend a few hours at the lake, Gideon had heard.

"She could probably use a hand," he told himself. "She could use a babysitter. You could make yourself useful."

He could say goodbye to the little one now as well, he acknowledged. He'd say his goodbyes to his sister when she left later this morning. Last night had been his farewell to Caroline. He wasn't going to touch her again or look back. Just a simple "thank you, goodbye, and have a wonderful life." He'd run into her now and then, of course. It was bound to happen. But they'd be past the wildly arcing electricity that crackled between them by then. He and Caroline would be fine. Absolutely fine…in time.

So all that was left was Libby. It was time to break the slender strings that had tied him to the baby. Just a few giggles and smiles and then Caroline would be done with her packing. Everything would be neatly wrapped up and ready to go.

He climbed the stairs to the room where Libby had made her nest these last few weeks. He peeked in and found her in her crib, standing on wobbly legs, rubbing her eyes. Caroline must have put her down for a nap while she packed. Obviously, his entrance had awakened her.

"Uh oh, angel, looks like I came at a bad time."

But she raised her arms to be picked up anyway.

He lifted her, snuggling her warm body close, and carried her to the rocker in the corner. "Let's see if we can't read you back to sleep," he suggested. "We need a story."

At the word "story," Libby's eyes rounded. She jabbered loudly and excitedly, pointing toward the shelves where Caroline obviously kept her books.

On the bottom shelf was an assortment of colorful picture books. Gideon knelt, baby on his hip, and picked out one called *If You Give a Mouse a Cookie*. Apparently this was one of Libby's favorites, because as he returned to the chair with her and turned the pages, reading quietly, she maintained a constant chorus of "mou," and "book," sometimes excitedly patting the pages. Her little body wiggled and squirmed with excitement as he read.

"Aunt Caroline has read this book to you before, eh, Princess?" he whispered.

At the mention of her aunt's name, Libby looked toward the door expectantly, and Gideon almost found himself looking, too, as if they could conjure the lady up just by looking.

"Sorry, sweetheart, she's getting ready to leave." The words felt heavy falling from his lips and Libby must have sensed his sadness, because she snuggled closer at that moment. She pressed her cheek up against his heart. For long moments they just sat there together, her sweet baby breath warming him, his heartbeat rhythmically sounding beneath her ear. Then Libby climbed from his lap and went over to the shelf. She brought back another book, but when Gideon tried to lift her onto his lap to read it, she simply giggled and danced away, trekking back to the shelf for another book and then another to hand him. Soon Gideon's lap contained a heavy stack of books.

As one of them slipped and fell, Libby squealed with laughter.

"You think you're pretty cute, don't you, sweetheart? Well...you're right," Gideon said, reaching out to nudge her nose with his thumb. She laughed and brought him another book. And yet another.

The pile on his lap was shifting. Gideon reached out to catch the sliding stack as Libby went back for more. And then he heard a small cry, a sickening thud, a nightmare sound. Sweeping the stack of books from his lap, he raced to Libby, but she had already reached up to grab another book and with the shifting, depleted stack of books, a heavy tome on the top shelf had lost its support and toppled. It had already crashed down on her, stealing her always tenuous balance, and she had fallen, hitting her head on the hard wooden floor.

She lay there, still and pale.

Gideon's heart and mind went into a blind free fall.

The next few minutes were a red blur. He probably did everything wrong. He wasn't even sure he remembered what happened other than that he had scooped the baby up and roared out Caroline's name as he took long, swooping strides down the hall.

Somehow she was there. Somehow he made her understand the nature of the emergency. And then the ambulance arrived. Caroline and Libby, still silent and so very small and limp, were tucked into its great cavernous space.

Gideon didn't remember driving to the hospital. He didn't notice much of anything until he got to the waiting room and saw Caroline there. Pacing. Endlessly pacing, her arms pulled in tightly against her body.

"Have you seen the doctor?" he managed to say, and

she looked up straight into his eyes. Without hesitation, she came into his arms, resting her face against his chest. He felt her nod, her soft hair snagging on his shirt.

He had done this. To her. And to a child. How could he have hurt them like this? And what could he do to make things easier for her now?

Gideon felt the emptiness of helplessness. All he could do was hold Caroline. It wasn't enough.

Caroline looked up into Gideon's eyes and she saw the depth of his despair written there. Concern ran deep. Guilt stood out on him like an aura.

''She's fine,'' she said softly. ''Since she's so small and the blow was to the head, they want to keep her overnight for observation to make sure there's nothing wrong. But I'm sure she'll come home in the morning. She'll be all right, Gideon. Libby's a hardy little thing.''

''I should have watched her more closely.''

''Gideon,'' Caroline whispered. ''It's impossible to foresee every accident, every possibility for danger with children. We try. We do our best to make their world as safe as we can, but things happen and sometimes they can't be prevented.''

''This could have been prevented if I'd been watching more closely.''

Caroline shook her head. ''She moves like a little roadrunner when she wants to.''

''Then I shouldn't have had books that heavy on that shelf.''

She took a deep breath, frowned. ''I know that shelf. None of the books are that heavy. She was probably just startled. It wasn't the book. It was the fall, and Gideon, babies fall all the time. You can't stop them from doing it. Even if you wanted to, you couldn't do it. It's how they learn balance and how they learn to get up and keep going.''

He took his hands from her back and held her from him. ''I'm sure that's true,'' he said softly, curving his palm around her cheek. But he didn't say more and she could tell by the rigid line of his body that she could say anything and everything, but it wouldn't make a difference. Gideon had already made up his mind.

''You're just going to punish yourself, aren't you?'' she asked. ''Long after Libby is back laughing and dancing around, you'll still be chastising yourself.''

He frowned. ''I don't intend to dwell on it, no.''

''You're lying. You have responsibility bred so deeply in your bones that it would be impossible for you not to beat yourself up about this.''

He raised one brow in that imperious, bored expression he affected so easily. It wasn't working this time. She knew it was a mask.

''She's going to be all right, Gideon. Children are very resilient.

''They shouldn't have to be.''

''Yes, they should. We protect them as much as we can, but when accidents happen, their very resiliency is how they survive and grow and learn.''

She was going to tell him that Libby might not even remember this incident in a few weeks, but the look he gave her stalled the words right in her throat. The truth was that Libby was young enough that she probably would forget quickly, but Gideon would never forget. No surprise. She wasn't sure that she herself would ever forget the tortured sound of his voice when he'd brought the baby to her. But this was different. Gideon believed that he was inherently incapable of caring enough to protect a child. He felt that some people shouldn't have the right to bear children, and maybe he was right. She was pretty darn sure that his parents hadn't deserved the privilege of raising him, especially if they had taught him to be so rigid in his expectations of himself.

"She's not unconscious now, Gideon. I've seen her. I'll stay with her tonight if I can, and tomorrow I'll bring her home. She'll be fine," she said more firmly. She tried to infuse all the sincerity and truth and caring that was in her soul into her voice and into her eyes when she looked up at him.

But his own eyes had gone still and cloudy. "Thank goodness," was all he said. "And Caroline?"

She never took her attention from him.

"I'm sorry, love," he said, and she was sure that he was talking about so much more than Libby. He was sorry for not being what she wanted him to be. He was sorry for all the intimacies they'd shared which could only lead so far. He was possibly sorry for hiring her in the first place. And he was sorry that their goodbye could not have gone more smoothly.

And she was sorry too. Sorry they had to say goodbye at all.

Chapter Eleven

Caroline was leaving. That thought played over and over in Gideon's mind the next day as they stood on the steps leading to his home. Her leaving wasn't a surprise. It was what they'd been working up to from the start. But his own reaction to losing her—the pain as fierce as fire that rose within him hadn't been something he'd planned. He wanted his calm emotionless life back, and yet he felt like he would never stop aching.

A pretty blond woman stopped on the landing. Libby's mother smiled down at her child as the baby blew smacking kisses toward Gideon. Libby. Another ache. He blew a kiss back.

"You can touch her," Caroline said softly. "You won't break her, you know. She's fine and healthy."

"I know. That's good." He did step forward then. He let the baby put her tiny arms around his neck. He kissed her soft cheek and swallowed the lump that lodged in his throat.

"Goodbye, angel," he told her.

She waved cheerily with both hands as her mother smiled back at him and carried her away. As if she were just going for a drive and would be back any moment.

He waved back and turned away.

Somewhere in his consciousness, he saw Roy carrying out the bags. Gideon heard the car door closing out on the drive. But mostly he just saw Caroline.

She looked up at him with those big, clear-blue eyes in that absolutely direct way she had, and she smiled sadly. "Gideon," she said slowly, softly. "I—well, I guess this is goodbye. And since it is, I just want to let you know that it's been a lot more fun than I first thought it would be. I've enjoyed getting to know this house."

The house. Not him. He knew she was avoiding the issue, because the truth was too hard to face. The truth was that they'd gotten to know each other better than they'd planned. He'd broken his own rules. Repeatedly. But right now he didn't care. She was leaving.

"And now you can tell Bobby Cummings he was wrong," he said, dredging up a small smile from somewhere deep inside him. She was doing her best to make him feel good. He was darn well going to do his best to make this easy for her as well. "You stayed in my house and Eldora didn't sink into the ground."

"Yes, I did, didn't I?" she agreed. She held out her hands.

He took them in his own.

"Thank you, Gideon," she whispered. "For letting me stay here. It really is a romantic, fairy-tale house. Not that I'm a romantic sort of woman, you know."

"Of course not. I'll deny it to anyone who says differently."

Caroline nodded and looked up at the man she had grown to love against her will. She needed to keep this simple. It was the deal, the way things had to be. And so she continued to smile politely. ''Still,'' she continued, ''I've enjoyed taking care of your house. I—well, I thought it was going to be just a little awful and scary doing this job for you, but it wasn't. It was…'' She paused, taking a deep and shaky breath. ''It was…''

He reached out and gently placed his fingers over her lips. ''It worked out well for both of us, I think.''

''Yes, and now you have your life back just as you wanted.''

He nodded. ''And you can go on with yours.''

She shifted from one foot to another. She slid her hands from his grasp. ''Have a good life, Gideon.''

''Yes. I will,'' he agreed. ''Be happy, Caroline.''

And then she turned. She had made it through the goodbye. She was leaving and she hadn't done one foolish thing—except her heart just wouldn't have it that way.

She quickly turned back and lifted her lips.

He stared down at her with those fierce, dark eyes of his. And then slowly he lowered his head. His lips barely brushed hers. She touched his arm. His muscles were tense, hard, and she knew that he was forcing himself to hold back.

He wanted to end things right. So did she, but for her, it was different. She loved him, she knew now that she would love him forever, and if this was to be the last time she kissed him, she wanted it to be more than this brief touch of her lips to his. So she rose on her toes. She wrapped her arms around his neck.

"Goodbye, Gideon," she whispered, her voice broken and raspy as she melted against his heart.

He caught her to him. He kissed her back, fiercely, possessively. With heat and strength, his fingers plunged into her hair.

Then, just as quickly, she pushed away.

"I'm sorry I brought Libby when it caused you so much pain," she whispered. "And I'm sorry I made you break your cardinal rule about not kissing the hired help, Gideon."

And then she stumbled down the stairs and flew into the car. In only seconds Gideon and his fairy-tale home had faded into the distance.

The apartment wasn't big, but it seemed huge and empty at the moment, Caroline thought three days later, trekking from one end to the other. She should be getting on with things, checking to see if Summerstaff had a list of employers who still had positions they wanted filled. She should be looking for some direction in her life. Silly to still be worrying if Gideon was working too hard, if Mrs. Williams was feeding him well, if he'd gone back to having an ice-cream-free freezer.

There were things to be done, books to write, flowers to plant. She should be starting her hunt for a husband.

"You're not getting any younger, Caroline O'Donald," she told herself. But instead of getting to any of those things she should be doing she dropped onto the sofa. She flipped through a magazine, not even seeing the photos, and wondered how long it would be before she would be able to get back to the idea of marrying and starting her family.

Nothing had really changed, after all. She'd fallen in

love, but she had always known that life with Gideon wasn't an option. Since she hadn't planned a marriage based on love, anyway, nothing should have changed. She could still have a friendly marriage, still have her babies.

Only every time she looked at a child these last few days, she saw Gideon kissing Libby goodbye. She saw him carrying Libby into her room and looking like he'd just murdered his own soul. She had taken a man who had *thought* himself unfit for fatherhood and had made him very *sure* he was unfit. This wasn't like the mistakes she'd made in her life before, the problems she'd sometimes caused with her impetuous ways. In those cases, life had always gone on as usual in spite of her follies.

This time she knew nothing would ever be the same. Gideon had gotten a taste of the joy of babies and had lost it just as quickly. She had found love and spoiled herself for any other man. There would be no marriage for her, no babies.

Sometimes life and love didn't give a person a choice. Sometimes a person's heart got in the way of their head and there was just nothing that could be done about it.

She was in love with Gideon Tremayne. She had fallen for the fairy tale after all, and it had not had a happy ending. But she was glad that she had loved him. No matter how painful this was, even though she would never have children, she just couldn't regret Gideon. If she had to spend all her life paying the price, he'd been worth it.

The thought almost brought a smile to her lips. She wondered what Gideon would think if he knew how much he'd changed her life. She'd finally realized that heroes really did exist. He'd restored her faith in romance, even if she'd never have her very own love story.

Someday, maybe she'd meet him on the street and she'd tell him so in a kind of friendly, impersonal way. Maybe they'd both smile and laugh about that, but not today. Today she just couldn't make herself smile.

She'd been gone three days and in those three days Gideon had walked every room of his house three thousand times. He'd thrown himself into work. He'd made plans to set up three new systems for three new companies. By rights he should be ecstatic, but today he was pacing the rooms of his house. He was listening for a voice and the sound of laughter that would never fill the air here ever again.

He was beginning to hate his home. It was missing something. Not ice cream. Mrs. Williams kept plenty of that. She talked about Caroline constantly. As if he needed to be reminded that the woman was living just across town, he thought, eyeing the flowers Mrs. Williams had started supplying now that Caroline had gone. He glanced at the wacky poster Caroline had hung on his wall and saw her face the day she had presented it to him. No, he didn't need to be reminded of anything concerning her. What he needed to do was forget her.

But she was here, in his house, in his thoughts, in his dreams. And those dreams. Caroline sliding under the sheets of his bed, Caroline with her lips pressed to his, Caroline with a baby in her arms. His baby. Their baby.

The ache around his heart intensified. It ran through his whole being.

He wanted her, and he wanted her child, too, he realized.

But that couldn't be. He was who he was. The past was still there.

His thoughts ballooned, almost forcing the feel of Caroline out. But not quite. The memory of her was strong, and in that sense, she was with him.

Children are resilient, he could almost hear her say. And yes, he supposed she was right. His parents had been cold, he thought, stilling his pacing. He had wrapped himself in a blanket of isolation to protect himself from it. He'd fought his pain by freezing his own emotions. But he had survived the ice, he realized, just as he realized that their coldness had its depths in something more. His parents had married for duty, and they'd both resented it. That resentment had spilled onto the lives of their children. He and Erin had always been a reminder of a marriage that should never have happened.

But my parents' ways aren't mine, he reminded himself, thinking of his work, the changes he'd made to his home, his very dreams. "I'm *not* my parents," he whispered. *I can learn to give love.* And as for Caroline, well, he could no more regret any time spent with her than he could imagine her treating their children as a duty—a mere means to carry on the Tremayne line. He could almost picture the fierce way she would look at him if he ever suggested such a thing. The very thought almost made him smile.

Almost.

Because she wasn't here. And he knew her. She had a purpose for her life. She had a goal. Lots of babies, with a man who would be a friend.

Maybe she'd already found the man. It could happen. With Caroline anything could happen. While he sat dreaming, she could be on her way down the aisle. She and some other man might be planning a family.

The thought nearly brought him to his knees. She wanted a man to marry. He wanted her for his own, and if he was ever to have her, he had to convince her that *he* was the right man for what she had in mind.

But how? He'd been very clear about what he wanted and didn't want, just as she had. She'd been hurt by men before. She might have been attracted to him, might have indulged in some scorching embraces, but the woman had insisted that she had no interest in any long-term romantic relationships.

"She's not a romantic woman," he whispered, picturing her waltzing around the ballroom in a long romantic gown with her hair drifting over her shoulders in long, silky tendrils. "She doesn't want love. What's a man who loves her to do?"

What was a man to do when his heart belonged to a woman like Caroline?

Hope, he thought. And more. Any man who loved Caroline would do everything he could for her. Including giving her up to another man if that was what would truly make her happy. Even if it broke his own heart in two.

"What we need here is help, Tremayne. From someone who knows her and who cares about her." And someone who would know a lot more about how to effect the plan he had in mind.

Gideon blew out a long breath. He picked up the telephone and began to dial.

She was only dragging her feet because the day was so hot, Caroline told herself two days later as she trudged down the baking sidewalk on her way home. It didn't have anything to do with the fact that she'd just gotten back from the first day at her new job and her boss was a kind, good-looking man of marriageable age, a family-type who had looked at her with interest. She was *sure* that it had little to do with the fact that she didn't have the least desire to pursue the matter, because Gideon had taken up permanent residence in her heart.

She was just—overly warm. She wanted a shower. She wanted to kick her shoes off and just sit in the back-yard and not think. Not about her new employer and most certainly not about the man who'd gone before him.

Caroline paused in front of her house. She closed her eyes to blot out the vision of Gideon that threatened to burst into her mind's eye. She didn't want to think about deep gray eyes or midnight hair or a voice that could make her want to weep with longing.

"Just stop it right now," she ordered herself. "You are going to march into the house, turn the water on full blast and wash every thought you have down the drain right now."

Creative visualization, that was the ticket.

But when she opened her eyes, instead of just seeing her street and her house, she was sure she saw a trio of horses coming down the tree-lined lane. In fact, she was positive that those were horses and riders. The strap of her purse slipped from her grip and she moved quickly to catch it, to step to her door and escape from this craziness, because there was definitely something famil-iar about one of those riders.

An ache rose up inside her. She saw Gideon in everything now. Would she ever stop seeing him, stop looking for him?

But as she stood there frozen in space and time, the riders drew nearer.

Caroline's breath caught high in her throat. Her heart started slamming against her chest.

"Gideon," she whispered.

He was mounted on a tall ebony horse with a white blaze down its face. Dressed all in black, from his tall boots, leggings and tunic to the long, flowing cape that swirled around him, Gideon was an imposing sight, a man from another era. His horse tossed its head, the silver on its bridle glinting in the sun. A sword rested in a scabbard that ran along the horse's side, together with a shield that sported the gold Tremayne crest. And then Gideon stopped a hundred feet away. His lips moved and one of the boys beside him nodded.

He dismounted and began to walk toward her.

Caroline curled her fingers closed into fists. She opened her mouth to speak, but words and anything resembling clear thought just flew away. Her breath died in her throat.

Gideon moved four long strides closer. His eyes were fixed on her, dark and compelling. Her heart was suddenly pounding, her thoughts were galloping around in circles.

He kept moving closer. And closer still. His gaze locked onto hers and she couldn't look away.

"Gideon?" she managed to say weakly when he was still a few feet away.

"Exactly," he said.

"You're here."

''That I am, love,'' he said gently. His voice was like a kiss, warm and deep and caressing.

''I—Gideon, why are you here? And why are you—'' She gestured to his clothing, to the horse.

''Ah, there's the question,'' he said, his lips lifting slightly. ''I'm here—'' He paused and moved a step closer, placing his lips near her ear. ''I'm here, Caroline, because I'm a man who's lost his heart and soul. I'm looking for a bride and it's very clear to me that only one woman will ever do.''

She closed her eyes, felt the world spinning.

''Caroline,'' he said softly, stepping even closer, fitting his palms to her arms, sliding his hands upwards in a slow caress. ''Are you all right, love? Am I upsetting you?''

She opened her eyes. ''You're confusing me,'' she whispered. She looked straight at his chest, at the soft dark cloth stretched taut over his muscles.

''It was my grandfather's,'' he said simply, by way of explanation. And then he said nothing else for long seconds. He cupped her face in his palms and just looked at her. He gazed into her eyes, holding her captive there with the warmth of his expression.

''Gideon,'' she finally whispered, ''I—''

He gently rubbed one thumb across her lips, stopping her speech as he shook his head slowly. Finally he smiled, just a bit. Wistfully, it seemed to her.

''I know you're not a romantic woman, Caroline, angel,'' he said, finishing on a deep sigh, ''and so I apologize, but it seems that I've recently discovered that I *am* a rather romantic man. I didn't think I could love. I didn't want to love, but then I met a lady. A very special lady. One who had me breaking all the rules I'd lived by all my life.''

She felt an embarrassing flush begin to steal up her cheeks. He was so close. The warmth of him was so enticing. She wanted to lean in and rest her cheek against his chest, but more than that she wanted him to keep on talking, keep on saying what he was saying. She wanted to be looking into his eyes while he said it. To know if his words could possibly be real. She'd heard talk of love from men before, not like these words coming from Gideon, who would never, ever lie to her or toy with her. Still, she wanted him to keep talking.

''I—I didn't plan to make you do anything you didn't want to.''

''You didn't,'' he said gently, reaching out to stroke her hair. ''Everything I did with you was something that I very much wanted to do, including losing my heart it seems. You own it, you know, love. Completely. And Caroline, I know that this doesn't fit in with your plans any more than you fit into the plans I once made, but do you think you could ever feel the same about me? Do you think—could it be possible—that you would ever consider me worthy to be the father of those children you plan on having?''

A mist of tears had her blinking, but she managed to smile up at him. She slid her hands beneath his cloak around his waist. ''You make a wonderful knight, you know. Even without the armor.''

''I didn't want to scrape your soft skin with rough metal,'' he confided gently.

She couldn't help it then. A single tear tracked down her cheek.

Gideon swore softly. ''I've made you cry.''

She shook her head. "No—I—" She snaked her palm up around his neck and held on.

Gideon sucked in a deep breath. "Caroline," he said on a groan. "I'm hoping this means—that is, love—oh love, I'm half crazy with wanting you. Do you think you could ever love me back?"

To answer she rose on her toes and planted a kiss on the hard line of his jaw. She breathed in deeply of the warm, clean scent of the man who'd been drifting through her dreams for so long. "I think I've loved you forever, Gideon. I have. And I'd already decided I couldn't marry for convenience, not when my heart was given for life. Besides," she said, as she leaned back to look at him and he wrapped his arms around her to hold her in place. "I *know* you'll make a wonderful father. I couldn't make babies with any other man."

His breath left his body in a long shudder and a smile finally lifted his lips.

"Caroline. Love. That's good. That's very good," he drawled in a low, sexy voice that rumbled through her body. "Because I have lots of rooms in my house. Plenty of rooms for children to sleep and to play. Plenty of rooms for a man and a woman to make love."

Lifting her into his arms, he turned and walked back toward the waiting horses. As they got closer, she saw that his page and squire weren't actually boys at all, but Emily and Rebecca, both of whom were beaming at her. As Gideon set Caroline down and took control of his mount, the two women waved at their friend.

"Not bad, Caroline," Emily called gaily.

"Looks good in tight pants and boots," Rebecca agreed with a grin.

Caroline grinned back at her friends. "I love you

both,'' she said. She knew that coming here today had been a sacrifice for her friends. Emily and Simon were just finding each other, falling in love, and Rebecca…well, Rebecca was still hurting, coming quickly to the end of her employment with Logan Brewster, Caroline feared. But they'd come because they cared, she thought, with love in her heart. She knew she'd never find better friends.

Or a man like Gideon. He moved forward, taking Emily's hand and then Rebecca's. ''Thank you, ladies. I'm in your debt forever,'' he said with a bow as he retrieved his horse. Rebecca and Emily waved goodbye. They slowly rode away.

Then Gideon was settling Caroline on his horse, swinging up behind her, and wrapping his arms about her. He held her close against his chest as they started back through town to the cheers of the crowd that had gathered to see the knight and his horse and the lady who loved him.

It was a very large crowd and a certain segment of it, led by a grinning Roy, trailed after them for a distance. A few calls of ''Sir Gideon'' rang out.

Caroline studied Gideon until he looked down and gave her a heartbreaking grin. Then she leaned back against him, reveling in the feel of being held against his heart. When they arrived at the house and he slid from the horse and reached up for her, she stared down at him. She fingered a bit of his cloak that was blowing about.

''You did this for me,'' she said solemnly. ''And I know how you feel about your family's heritage. Duty and the Tremayne history has taken its toll on your happiness. I know it's caused you pain in the past. I don't want you to...to be sorry for anything, Gideon.''

He stared back at her with clear gray eyes. Taking her hand in his own, he turned it gently and kissed her palm. Slowly. Deliberately. He held her gaze with his own. ''I don't regret a single moment I've ever spent with you,'' he confided. ''Caroline love, I'd do anything for you with no regrets. Any time we spend together is precious to me, no matter what we do.''

She felt something tight within her chest ease. She smiled down at this man she loved so very completely.

''Then kiss me, Gideon. Love me.''

''I intend to, Caroline. My love, my heart, my lady forever.''

As she slid down off the horse, he lowered his head, touching his lips to hers and folding her into his arms where she intended to stay for the rest of her days.

Epilogue

Caroline lay back in the pillows in the big master bedroom at Tremayne Hall. Her hair lay in a loose curtain around her and her husband lay beside her.

"You're looking more beautiful than ever tonight, love," Gideon said, leaning over to pull her close as he kissed her lips. "Pregnancy must agree with you."

"And with you?" she asked with an anxious smile. "I suppose I should tell you that the doctor thinks it may be twins, although it's still too early to tell. I'm just getting so big so fast."

"Caroline?" he said, nibbling on her jaw as he flicked open the buttons on her nightgown. He smiled into her eyes for a brief second, a fierce gleam in his gaze.

"Yes?"

"You've just made me ecstatically happy," he said, emotion coloring his voice. "The happiest of men. I'll always feel blessed in finding you. You're beautiful in every way," he repeated. "And you'll be more breathtakingly beautiful when you're nine months large with our babies.''

"I love when you say things like that," she said dreamily.

"And I love you, sweetheart. Eternally," he said as he lazily began to drift down her body, kissing her throat, her breasts. As he touched his lips to the sensitive skin of her stomach, he paused.

"This is where our baby is," he said with wonder, as if it had never occurred to him before. "I can't believe I ever thought I didn't want children. I can't wait to see you with our babies in your arms. I'm going to be a good father, Caroline."

At his words, filled with deep emotion and promise, she reached down and pulled him up beside her. She molded her lips to his and he could feel the taste of sweet tears on her mouth. "You *are* a wonderful father, my love. I'm sure Libby loves you like one and you're so good with her."

He kissed her back and then grinned at her when they finally parted. "Would you mind telling Erin that then, please. She's been reading baby books like crazy and giving me all kinds of tips on what I should do when our children arrive. I only wonder how much more of that Brandon has to listen to."

"He loves it," Caroline said with a confident smile. "Who would have thought that short little visit would have resulted in so much happiness? You. Me. Brandon following Erin back home and wooing her until she was silly with love. I'm so happy that you and your sister are going to both become parents just two months apart, Gideon. I love happy endings."

She pushed herself farther into Gideon's arms and snuggled close to him.

"Then let's make one, love. Let's make another happy ending tonight," he said, his voice low and husky, "because much as I enjoy discussing my sister's happiness, right now I can't wait to make love with the woman of my heart."

He touched her gently, oh so gently, as he stroked her.

Caroline closed her eyes, and sighed.

"Oh yes, Gideon, let's do that. You make the most wonderful happy endings, my love. The very best."

Gideon smiled as he pulled his oh-so-romantic wife into his arms and feasted on her lips.

* * * * *

MILLS & BOON®

Makes any time special™

Mills & Boon publish 29 new titles every month. Select from...

Modern Romance™   Tender Romance™

Sensual Romance™

Medical Romance™   Historical Romance™

MAT2

A Perfect Family

An enthralling family saga by bestselling author

PENNY JORDAN

Published 20th July

*Available at branches of WH Smith, Tesco,
Martins, RS McCall, Forbuoys, Borders, Easons,
Sainsbury, Woolworth and most good paperback bookshops*

4 FREE
books and a surprise gift!

We would like to take this opportunity to thank you for reading this Mills & Boon® book by offering you the chance to take FOUR more specially selected titles from the Modern Romance™ series absolutely FREE! We're also making this offer to introduce you to the benefits of the Reader Service™—

- ★ FREE home delivery
- ★ FREE gifts and competitions
- ★ FREE monthly Newsletter
- ★ Exclusive Reader Service discounts
- ★ Books available before they're in the shops

Accepting these FREE books and gift places you under no obligation to buy, you may cancel at any time, even after receiving your free shipment. Simply complete your details below and return the entire page to the address below. *You don't even need a stamp!*

YES! Please send me 4 free Modern Romance books and a surprise gift. I understand that unless you hear from me, I will receive 6 superb new titles every month for just £2.49 each, postage and packing free. I am under no obligation to purchase any books and may cancel my subscription at any time. The free books and gift will be mine to keep in any case.

P1ZEA

Ms/Mrs/Miss/Mr ....Initials......................................
BLOCK CAPITALS PLEASE

Surname ....

Address ....

....

....Postcode....................................

Send this whole page to:
UK: FREEPOST CN81, Croydon, CR9 3WZ
EIRE: PO Box 4546, Kilcock, County Kildare (stamp required)